Press Pause

Relax with a poem

By the Cafe Writers of Rugby

EDITED BY JOHN HOWES AND FRAN NEATHERWAY

Introduction

POETRY: WHAT'S THE POINT?

I remember asking my seven-year-old son for his opinion of poetry.

"It sucks," he said, profoundly, obviously not that impressed.

Well, I can understand where he was coming from. Poetry is not an easy sell. People seem to prefer stories. When we sell our work at book festivals, you can see customers gravitating towards the stories, especially the novels. Poetry is perhaps perceived as elitist, too dense to understand, and not a satisfying experience.

But I have found that, if you give it a chance, poetry can be incredibly rewarding. Indeed, often with a poem, you are getting an insight deep into the mind of an individual who is saying something which regular prose cannot convey.

The other great strength of poetry is its brevity. You don't need to use too many words and you don't need to read too many words. Like the lyrics of a great song, there is so much beneath the surface and, often, the writer will let you draw your own conclusions. She or he will not spell everything out - and rightly so. If it were all too obvious, there would be no mystery, nothing to talk about, nothing to think over or bring you back for a second reading.

When I was teaching, I found that children quickly warmed to the skill of writing poetry. They liked the fact that there were no rules. I used to tell them - don't worry about rhymes, don't worry about punctuation, don't worry about spelling. Just write something you feel. Tell us what you love or what makes you angry. Find your poetic voice!

Hopefully, within the pages of our first poetry-only anthology, you will find something to make you think, occasionally smile, and perhaps shed a tear. We have a varied and talented group of people in the Rugby Cafe Writers. Some of our poets enjoy the rigour of writing rules - and you will find in these pages examples of carefully written poetry with syllables counted and rhyming schemes strictly followed.

It is fun to do this and we can admire the skill of poets who choose these popular formats.

Others, though, prefer free verse, just writing what they think and feel without a set structure in mind. Either approach is fine and to be enjoyed. In poetry, there are no wrong answers!

Some of the poems here were the result of a shared writing challenge in which we were all given a title or topic to reflect on. For instance, you will find several poems here about a character called 'Ferdinand', a name we were all given as a challenge to create a character. Similarly, you will find plenty of poetry about cats, but not so much about dogs.

We have grouped the poems loosely into six themes and we hope you enjoy the way they flow together. On occasions, we have asked the poet to write an introductory sentence to say what inspired that particular poem.

And if you enjoy the poetry, why not have a go yourself? Join a local group of writers, discover your poetic voice and share your poems. It could make you feel so much better.

John Howes, Rugby Cafe Writers
www.rugbycafewriters.com

INDEX

PEOPLE

THE JEALOUS BROTHER

That winter's day the rain poured down
with freezing sleet and hail.
It changed the footpaths into mud
and flooded all the dale.

But William had a girl to meet,
whatever was the weather,
a girl he met nine months ago
and tumbled in the heather.

But this girl lived ten miles away
without a gentle mother,
without a father's loving care
but with her jealous brother.

William wore his shepherd's cloak
and boots upon his feet
for he must fight the rain and hail
his darling for to meet.

He crossed the dales and climbed the fell,
a stony path and steep.
He took the path across the moor
where the bog was deep.

In a cottage poor and cold
his little son was born.
Before the child was one hour old
from his mother's arms he was torn.

Her brother held the child's throat,
he took his cold, sharp knife
and there beside his sister's bed
he took the baby's life.

She left her bed, she left the room,
went out in her nightgown
and in the raging river deep
this grieving girl did drown.

And on the moor her lover's life
was lost in this foul weather
and there they walk on winter nights
hand in hand together.

Wendy Goulstone

CHRIS

The phone rings in the dead of night.
I rush downstairs alarmed.
It's Chris! shouts an excited voice.
It's a boy! I'm a father!

I congratulate Chris.
Great news, I say. What's the name?
Felix, he says, ecstatically.

You must be happy, I say.
Chris agrees and, falteringly, says goodnight.
See you around, I mutter.

I wander back to bed, thinking.
Who the bloody hell is Chris?

John Howes

MEMORIES OF JOYCE

A sonnet

I stand before the old familiar door,
Three decades' worth of visits made before.
I hear the heavy footsteps cross the floor.
'Come in,' says Keith. 'Our Joyce is round the back.
She's sitting in the sun. She likes it there.
Our Jason's brood is with her, round her chair.'
A smile for him; for me a vacant stare.
'Remembering who folk are, she's lost the knack.'
He prompts her who I am: 'Your friend, Christine.'
'Have you come far?' she asks, just like a queen.
I hesitate. I can't speak what I mean.
I drink some tea and munch the proffered snack
And chatting, stay a while to show I care
For Joyce who wasn't in when I went there.

Chris Rowe

YOU, ME AND LIFE

You, Me and Gloria
We've known pain in our lives
But as we stood there
On the edge
Girlfriend!
We sang "I will survive"

You, Me and Tina
We've been punched, and scratched and bit!
So, we packed our bags
And walked
Girlfriend!
Singing "What's love got to do with it?"

You, Me and Maya
We stood strong, with heads
Held high.
And when life knocked us down
Girlfriend!
We shouted "Still I rise!"

Linda Slate

THE MAN ON THE TUBE

He came over and shook my hand.
Oh no, not him again, I thought.
The weirdo that always finds me.
Any shape or size, he always locks into my radar.
He told me his story.
The true, genuine sadness in his eyes just touched
my heart.
He no longer needed to tell me his story anymore,
as his eyes told me all that his heart felt.
My life flashed before my own eyes,
and I suddenly realised how life was
and how life could have been.
As my train arrived, I said goodbye,
so saddened by the painful soul I left behind.
I looked back, while the doors closed,
and I saw the sorrowful desperation
stare through those drunken eyes, and my tears
ran free.
And they did not stop.
The bottle had been opened.
One that I did not even know existed.
The waters ran free, and they poured out for hours.
I am left empty, relieved and free.
Goodbye, Dan.
How I wish I could have helped you,
just as you have helped me.

Lindsay Woodward

MY MUM

Special,
She said as she lay dying.
You always were the special one.
Neatly hoovered every morning.

And,
As I flushed away the morphine,
I thought of John the Milkman.
He was a smackhead too.
Just like mum.

Afterwards we posed for photos
like it was a celebration of death.
Not a wake.
The vicar's black cowl flapping like bat's wings
in the bright spring air.

Simon Grenville

DONNA

There you were,
Standing by the backdoor of the office
Smoking a cigarette, looking glum.
I approached from the car park,
Mumbled good morning and went up to work.

I didn't ask how you were doing.
I didn't pass the time of day.
I didn't take a moment to enter your moment,
Spare a minute to plumb your depths,
To draw out the truths troubling your mind,
The demons dragging you down.

Then that night,
You took your own life,
Ended your nightmare -
And it was too late to say 'how are you?'
Too late to give a workmate the chance
To say: This is why.

John Howes

THE SONG OF BERNARDO

*Bernardo, who speaks the first line of Hamlet, tells
Horatio of the ghost he has seen and that it looks like
the late king. When it reappears and then leaves, he is
the one to say 'See, it stalks away' which I echo in the
poem. He suggests it might be something to do with
'the present wars'. He seems well-informed but,
curiously, he is not there when Hamlet is taken to see
the ghost. Perhaps he decides it's safer not to know too
much...*

Without a sound
It turned around
And slowly stalked away

But what it meant
Or where it went
I can't afford to say.

Though it had gone
Our prince went on –
Came back in disarray.

I kept my mind
And stayed behind,
Spear-holder in this play.

He called it Dad,
But came back mad –
All ended in affray.

The Nobs got killed:
Their hearts are stilled.
But here on guard I stay.

And I'll survive
And stay alive:
I hear and I obey.

I stand up here
And hold my spear.
Our king's now from Norway.

At Elsinore
Now work's a bore,
But brought in reg'lar pay.

Then comes the night –
Horrendous fright –
Prince Hamlet blocked my way.

In trembling fear
I clutched my spear,
Cursed him who'd gone astray.

Without a sound
He turned around
And fading walked away.

Chris Rowe

TWO FASCINATING FERDINANDS

*Ferdinand – from Ferdinando, a name the Spanish
nicked from the Germans sometime before the 15th
century. It contains the words fardi "journey" and nand
"daring, brave".*

Ferdinand Magellan (1480-1521)

Ferdinand Magellan
Had adventures worth the tellin'
For he spent his life upon the seven seas
He was no spineless wimp,
And though hampered by a limp
Every chance for exploration he would seize

In 1517
He set out for the Philippines
His fleet sailing boldly to the west
He was the first to navigate
The treacherous Magellan Strait
Named in honour of his brave and daring quest

He journeyed 'cross the Pacific,
Towards the southern tropic
But met his fate in tribal conflagration
One vessel returned to Spain,
So we remember Magellan's name
For the first ever circumnavigation

Steve Redshaw

TWO FASCINATING FERDINANDS

Ferdinand Porsche (1875–1951)

Ferdinand Porsche
Built cars of course
He possessed a remarkable ability
From a very early age
He was totally engaged
By a fascination for electricity

In 1931,
Working with his son,
(Who, incidentally, was also Ferdinand)
Founded his company
And from its factory
Created his world-famous brand

In 1934,
Before the dark days of war,
The iconic Beetle made its appearance
Father and son, the ideal team,
Made Porsche the motor-car dream
The pinnacle of driving experience

Steve Redshaw

COURAGE I ONCE KNEW

Her hair was black as mystery,
Her eyes enquiry blue,
Her skirt was a mix of earth and sky
and colours I once knew.

Her skin glowed bright by candlelight
as she peered into my palm,
And said that I could risk it all
and never come to harm.

There in her room of ancient hues,
With carpets on the wall,
She mumbled words from long ago
into her crystal ball.

"Time is short, the journey long,"
She whispered to my face,
"Begin tonight and go with speed,
And never slow the pace."

The handsome woman touched my arm,
Her smile warm as the sun,
"A sign will show you where to start,
And where your feet should run."

In my lower vertebrae,
I felt a burning fuse,
Adventure called and I would go,
But first a few more clues.

"How will I know which way to turn?"
She smiled and touched my chin,
Then looked into my eyes and said,
"Directions lie within.

"You'll know the way, you'll find the means,
We each have our own song,
To guide us on the quest of life
and keep the spirit strong.

"Yet most will never give it voice
and when their days are done,
It's buried with them in the grave
Their song of life unsung."

There was no more to hear that night,
I knew I had to leave,
And find a life whose cloth contained,
More colours in the weave.

The woman stood and shook my hand,
I paid her more than fair,
The answers she had given me I'd
always known were there.

That as the years go by we find,
The rainbows of our youth,
Fade to pastel then to grey,
And mock us with the truth.

It's not the pressures on your life,
It's not the things you do,
It's only being too scared to dream
that builds a cage for you.

Her hair was black as mystery,
Her eyes enquiry blue,
I gave coins, she gave me back,
The courage I once knew.

Geoff Hill

ALBERT

He was clever but little for his age
Held back in school at every stage
His father was from Timbuktu in Mali
His mother, from Leeds, celebrated Diwali
Granny followed either Pope
Uncle Robert thought it all a joke
Albert didn't get it

At school, most things were fun
But if his homework wasn't done
Teacher said Jesus the Lord
Couldn't copy from the board
Football practice against the grammar
Posh side of town "the Thomas Cranmer"
Protestant was just a label
Quizzed after the match they were able
To answer simple questions about prayer
He slumped back in his console chair
Albert didn't get it

Mum smiled Krishna calm
Her touch on his back a healing balm
"You'll have more patience
After another 50 incarnations"
Dad prayed five times a day
Quickly in his own way
"I met your mum when she was travelling
His prayer mat unravelling
"She has so many gods of course
Mohammed had a flying horse!"
Albert did not get it

Albert relied on his grandmother
For a view unlike any other
She could usually be found in a garden glade
Roman wisdom was her trade
Granny, so wise and smiled so wide
Heart as big as the September sky
"In the name of god above
I bask in our Holy Fathers' eternal love"
Then she died.

Uncle Bob at her cremation
Addressed the diverse congregation
"My mom loved watching the bees
Little beads stringing life around the flowers
We would walk around the mahonias and maple
trees
marvelled and meandered away the hours."
Life, wild or tame, strives
My confused and inquisitive boy
We are the owners of our own lives
The harvesters of our own joy
Every time I shake your hand
I say pleased to meet you in my mind
People are reaching in every land
To work together, to be kind
Albert finally got it.

Chris Wright

EVERYONE FELL ABOUT LAUGHING

Clary was on the press trip of a lifetime:
'Afternoon tea in Harrods' with a write-up
A *Vogue* magazine journalist
with a First Class train ticket.
She loved feeling special and looked the part.
Her hair recently coiffured, new glossy purple nails
Tight-fitting, black thigh-length boots,
A too-expensive designer purple coat.
Walking with difficulty in her too-high stilettos,
Wondering why she hadn't worn more comfy shoes
For travelling on public transport.

She surveyed the train looking for talent.
There directly opposite the train aisle
was *the* most gorgeous hunk,
A tall, blond and long-haired fella
who was walking towards her.
He sat down at a table
on the opposite side of the aisle.
He spoke: "What's your name, you lovely lady?"
She felt her mouth open to speak,
close and then whispered,
"I'm Clary, what's yours?"
"I'll have a g&t if you don't mind?"
"Oh, I meant what's your name?"
she said more loudly,
Louder than she meant to
and two older, rather serious-looking ladies
sitting at the table her hunk had moved from,
to be nearer her, scowled and whispered.
Her hunk stood up straight,
at least 6 feet 3 lovely inches tall,

He sat down next to Clary.
Looking even more handsome close to her,
he answered, "I'm Barry. What a pair we make,
Clary and Barry!"
The two older ladies sniggered.
"Are you going to London, Clary?"
"Yes, I am," she answered,
too overcome by Barry's deep, sexy voice.
"And where, lovely Clary,
will you be going to in London?"
"I'm going for Afternoon Tea in Harrods.
Would you like to join me?"
The two shocked ladies sat motionless,
their jaws dropped.
"I would love to join you in Harrods.
What time exactly?"

He beamed, enjoying her embarrassment,
she had blushed a beetroot red.
Then she said something absurd
and regretted it immediately, "I love you."
The older ladies gasped
and Barry leant towards Clary,
And planted a soft lingering kiss
on her rosy red cheek.
"Ladies, would you like a kiss on your cheek?
Meet my girlfriend, Clary. We are travelling actors.
Please buy tickets for our performance of
Clary and Barry, it's on tonight, 7pm,
The Traveller's Playhouse."

Everyone in the train carriage fell about laughing!

Kate A.Harris

THE BOY ON THE SAND

*This poem was inspired by a photograph my youngest
daughter took of her son on the sand, at Minehead.*

It's nine in the morning
On a bright late-October day
There are miles of empty sky, sea and sand
And one lone child, digging

He's stood on the wet sand
And the hole fills with water
Faster than he can empty it out
But he's smiling, happy

Trousers rolled up knee high
Thick coat with a hood, and hat
Bucket at his feet, and spade in hand
Oblivious to all

There is one more figure
Standing alone on the beach
Some way off from her madcap offspring
Where the sand is still dry

The morning air is hushed
His feet plash in the wet sand
The wide, blue sky goes on forever
To the sound of giggles

EE Blythe

THIS MAN

In memory of my father-in-law,
George Keith Biddle (1931-2015)

This man, this torrent of love, glowing in
Radiance and warmth, explosive in laughter,
Bearhugs and cheer, singing songs into life.
This man of England, this man of France, this
Man of words, language and celebration.
A star of our past, gone from our present,
But alive in all our futures, this man.

John Howes

FERDINAND THE MAN

Not Ferdi man, Ferdinand The Man
Dissin' me don't apply, fool
The game we're playin' is my rules
Schooled in Tulse Hill, tooled up in Brixton
Respect me man, while you can
Or you will be short one vixen
You yakety yak behind my back
But you can't take me down
I'm Ferdinand, The Man, it's my crown

Madalyn Morgan

GRACE

I'd taken the Northern Line down to Embankment
and walked across the bridge to the Festival Hall.
This was one of my favourite places for coffee,
looking out along the Thames,
watching the people go by.

Grace had already sent a message
saying she would be late.
I was in a quandary - to get the coffees in
and risk them being cold,
or to sit there, in a desirable spot,
with nothing on the table in front of me
except a telephone and The Guardian.
I opted to wait.
It was a dull day.
The river was grey but magnificent.
A dredging barge glided by at a funereal pace.
The cops sped in the opposite direction,
their solitary blue light flashing.
Body in the water, I assumed.
The minutes ticked away.

Then, there she was.
The sun appeared,
the lightning flashed,
fireworks filled the air,
the band struck up a glorious anthem.
Grace was here, smiling,
wonderfully disorganised as ever,
shoulder bag bursting with books.
Between lectures.
"Hi, dad," she said.

Let the heavens be praised
for the daughter I never had.

John Howes

LOCKDOWN TEA WITH JONATHAN AND MR B

I went out today without mask or gloves.
For lunch with Jonathan and Mr B.
I found them in the garden in the sun
What fun we had, we motley three.

Jonathan fetched the sandwiches;
Egg and cress on homemade bread.
And Mr B uncorked the wine –
A rosé and a red.

I chose rosé, Mr B did too, but Jonathan
With a more discerning palate had Sangiovese.
Relaxing in the garden, distanced of course,
We forgot for a while the madness of those days.

As if on cue when it was time to leave
clouds put the garden in shade.
Still distanced, we made steeples of our hands,
blew kisses and said goodbye.

Walking home it began to rain,
I lifted my face and closed my eyes.
It was good to be out again.
It was good to see those guys.

Madalyn Morgan

LIMERICK

An aspiring young lady from Hinckley
With plum in her mouth spoke distinc'ly,
But alas all too soon
It turned into a prune
Creating a well-spoken Wrinkly

Chris Rowe

WILLIAM THE THIRD

The gentleman in the velvet waistcoat

Once upon a time a gentleman in velvet
Sought to make his mark royally
By creating earthworks in Kensington
That horses wouldn't see
Satisfied with his labours
Ready for a nap
Ready for Sorrel
Her mount, his neck to snap
On the eighth day of March
In 1702 William the third passed away
It still provides mirth
They thank the gentleman
In waistcoat black
Sleeping between the earth

Paul Clark

GEORGE ON ONE LEG

*In memory of our great friend Peter Maudsley, a
member of Rugby Cafe Writers, who died in 2023.*

George Peter my opponent
Definitely religious always with a kind word or two
Evangelical Anglican irreverent
His real name was the last thing I knew

To everyone George was a friend indeed
No one's opinion esteemed higher.
I sometimes questioned the creed.
Who was I to pour cold water on a fire?

I'm sceptical and he was ecumenical.
I would enter the church and shout "where's
Peter?"
Which cheered up the funeral.
I was ejected by the greeter

George was bright and funny with it.
Outside the Thai restaurant we discussed exercise
"See if you can stand on one leg for half a minute,
 Chris, now close your eyes."

This morning again I wobbled like a jelly.
Ten second record in front
Of early morning telly
I duplicate the silly stunt

Long ago I saw a squirrel jump from a birch
It stood on one leg on a gravestone
Rodent nose twitched and on with the search
Our lives have meaning of their own.

Chris Wright

RAIN FALLS

The rain falls from her slate grey eyes
And soaks into the gentle bosom of the land
The wide green sea is empty of all souls
No-one comes to rescue, and comfort

The hills roll down to the water, as if to drink
The birds nestle in trees and hedges
Fox is in her den, and Badger's in his sett
Nothing calls, nothing moves, nothing sees

A half floating bundle, sodden and dark
Rocking backwards and forwards in the wash
Streamers of hair and weed, waving in the flow
Nothing to see the end of the sorrow

The rain falls on her slate grey eyes

EE Blythe

GLYN'S GOODBYE

It was overcast with grey.
That day.
And finding the place,
It was
(you may say)
Satisfactory.

Like they say
It was clean,
Freshly
still wet to the touch
Concrete.

In a wilderness still to be yet tamed.
Brambles that caught underfoot.
And snarled my shoe.

People queued as if at the cinema.
Mumbling politely.
Some in black.
Some in blue.
Very few that I knew
400 all told.
That's a lot.
I thought.
But I didn't count,
I didn't have my clicker.
Why should I?

I was there to say Goodbye to Glyn,
Never a friend,
But more than an acquaintance
If you see what I mean.

It's a funny thing with men,
They edge silently closer
To each other
Over time
As if afraid to touch closer
Their inner selves
And then share.

Four hundred folk
Stamping in the damp air.
But
He made a triumphant entrance,
Carried proudly before us.
And then lay quietly
In the corner.
While we chatted around him.

This man.
His life,
A stain on the silence
I think.
"Is he dead?"
"I bloody well hope so.
He'll have a hell of a shock
If he isn't nailed down tight."

A man I saw every day
A man now dead.
A man walking his dog in the cemetery.
While I learned my lines,
He walked the dog.
while I did funny accents,
He walked the dog
While I worried about my overdraft.
He walked the dog.
While I worried about my fear
Of intimacy,
He nursed his marriage.

How little I knew about him.
An MA from Warwick
A degree in classics
And remembered a millennium later.
For a one-handed catch at cricket.
How could an MA from Warwick
Go camping in the lake district,
And not remember a tin opener.
He did.
The two of them
Sharpish,
On the train back home
That same day.

Now I have a O-level in sociology
Grade Six.
And I know about tin openers!

I was a scout leader.
Woodpecker patrol,
Woodbridge
And fondly remembered
those endless Suffolk lanes of childhood,
Warm stretched days of heat.
And the soft, soft glow of the six o'clock sun
setting.

I spent a summers day with him once,
In the Seven Stars,
Watching the light fade
And walking back
Later,
Slightly more intimate than before.

Men are like that.
Slow to reveal.
I am used to it now.
But then it was new.

This slow disclosure.

And as we walked home,
There seeped from him a sadness,
A longing for something else,
Not quite defined.

Simon Grenville

WELSH FUNERAL

In memory of Mike. A funeral like no other.

Rods of rain relentlessly
Penetrating broad black shoulders
Carrying the coffin through the long grasses.
Smoothed back hair releasing
Ice cold droplets
Into necks' receptacles.
The burly bishop, the clergy and the family
Tumble into the church, overwhelmed
By arrival and dryness and light and trumpet sound.
Then the fireworks begin:
Shooting stars of words trailing red sparks
Of power, whole gold bars of words
Worth their weight and more.
Sure hope of resurrection.
Though he be dead
Yet shall he live.
And the noise and the glory
Of the words
Pour out over us all -
Standing there though we are
With damp feet
Wishing we could stamp
And spaniel shake ourselves.

Sylvia Mandeville

THE VICAR OF DUBLIN

Just scribbled today before lunch.
And again, in trouble
Shamus drank so much,
First a stout then a double.
He thought he was the Vicar of Dublin.
His donkey jacket was a vestment,
master of both testaments,
repulsed Attila the Hun,
saved the children of Carcassonne.
Lectured St Augustine about shyness
and gave a sandwich to Thomas Aquinas.
Like a colossus he strode across the walls of
history.
His friends walked him out into the Londonderry air.
Faith and the Mountains donated fog.
Stolen lambs out of mind
Far from Ebrington Square
Quoting from St Mark
He blessed the cats.
He blessed the rats.
He threw up over a dog
"I never ate that".
He passed out in the park
and the Mass still a mystery.

Chris Wright

POOR WOMEN

Shopping, daily, food selection
Preparing, waste not – want not
Cooking, endless days of making meals
Boiling, frying, baking, roasting
Balancing the housekeeping against needs
Desperately trying to achieve the wants
Especially at Christmas
And small ones' birthdays

Mending, making everything last
Sore fingers from darning, hand sewing new
garments
Long into the night, ready for next day
Repairing the damage of daily wear and tear
Passing altered clothing down through the ages
Making it look passable, hopefully acceptable
Accusations from the youngest, they never get new
Are barbs through the heart

Cleaning, the endless chore
Back-breaking, demoralising, harsh
Sweeping and mopping, open windows to dry
Red raw hands scrubbing bare wood floors
Dragging carpets and rugs outside to beat
Dusting, polishing, bees wax for the wood
Black-leading the grate, Cardinal Red the hearth
Removing the tarnish from brass

Daily scrubbing the front door step

Washing, laundry, the little blue bag
Struggle to hang out sodden sheets and nappies
Judged on the whiteness, the removal of stains
Telling tales of household secrets so shameful
Blocks of carbolic soap, boxes of soap flakes
Hand washing woollens, and trousers, and skirts
Soaking handkerchiefs in salt water to remove the
slime
Bleaching, starching, drying, ironing, fold and away

Not so very long ago

EE Blythe

REFUGEE

(Song lyrics)

Refugee, fleeing from your homeland,
Refugee, running through the night,
Refugee, seeking a new land,
Freedom may come with morning light,
Freedom may come with morning light

In your villages and towns the soldiers cut you down
Beating out revenge with bayonet and gun
As the blood of the innocents stain the sacred ground
The cries of your children linger on

Refugee, fleeing from your homeland,
Refugee, running through the night,
Refugee, seeking a new land,
Freedom may come with morning light,
Freedom may come with morning light

They would take it all, your body, mind and soul
They hide behind the lie that God is in control
Demanding your obedience, denying every right
Justifying cruelty and might

Refugee, fleeing from your homeland,
Refugee, running through the night,
Refugee, seeking a new land,
Freedom may come with morning light,
Freedom may come with morning light

You have set your mind on a hope that you will find
A life that gives you more than the one you leave behind
Escaping persecution, the hunger and the pain
Seeking a chance to live again

Refugee, straying from a known land
Refugee, stranger in a strange land
Refugee, straying from a known land
Refugee, stranger in a strange land

Refugee, fleeing from your homeland,
Refugee, running through the night,
Refugee, seeking a new land,
Freedom may come with morning light,
Freedom may come with morning light

Many dangers you will face as you seek your breathing space
But the memories you bear, that you cannot erase,
Fan the flames of desire and sow the seeds of hope
You make your way towards the morning light
Journeying towards the morning light

Refugee, fleeing from your homeland,
Refugee, running through the night,
Refugee, seeking a new land,
Freedom may come with morning light,
Freedom may come with morning light

May freedom come like morning light....

Steve Redshaw

PRECIOUS WASTE

Written in response to a news item, where three girls from Pakistan were raped and abused and hanged.

Three girls hanging from a tree,
In a far-off land.
Defiled.
Degraded.
Devalued.
Dead!
Like that one precious plate
Worth a king's ransom.
Dropped, cracked and splintered across the beauty,
Lying on the ground in harsh jagged patterns.
Of no value now.
Worthless.
May as well throw it away.
Throw the whole set away
It's no good with a piece missing

Linda Slate

FERDINAND

Ferdinand was a little boy
of barely four years old.
He liked to jump in puddles
and he didn't feel the cold,
He hadn't any siblings
and he sometimes wished he had
but he didn't think it was
the sort of thing that he could ask his dad.
Ferdinand was a little boy
of barely four years old
with his future all ahead of him
and adventures yet untold.

Ruth Hughes

LEAP YEAR 2024

An American man called Jed
his love life was very very busy
He didn't want to be wed
His latest flame was called Lindsay
She tracked him to a bar *Hillary's Hideway*
She found the partisan politics a bore
But he followed the election every day
And this was 2024
She got the idea from the TV
all the political stations
her man staring enthusiastically
and from her own impatience
"Jed, you say you love me but you love the election more.
If a Democrat is chosen you come to the altar with a smile,
if the Republicans win I'll walk out the door."
The bartender was listening the whole while,
his girlfriend was the local news presenter,
and before you could say "bridal lace work"
the deal was all over the Metro Centre.
The story, viral, infected the network,
New York cabbies argued Jed's case,
where Angelinos loved Lindsay the romantic
DC talk shows ignored the main race.
Fox news Sally was almost frantic.

Pennsylvania released a million balloons -
"Jed for Lindsay" - a logo with gold doves,
Chicago Tribune published satirical cartoons
Red voters in Carolina switched in droves.

You can probably guess, come November,
The Lovers could not walk down the avenue
Without having to remember
Their albatross media retinue.

All plays end; even the absurd,
Soon the 'X's were all counted like kisses,
Jed was as good as his word,
He lost his qualms about being Mr to Lindsay's Mrs.

And their syndicated wedding on Christmas Eve,
the US applauded with respect,
had a matron of honour you could not believe
the new Democratic lady president elect.

Chris Wright

PLACES

MY AFRICA

A dusty road and a heavy pack,
Weary feet and an aching back,
Sunburnt skin and lips that crack,
That's Africa to me.

Heat that comes from a blazing sun,
Humidity that's next to none,
A prayer for rain that does not come,
That's Africa to me.

A land of dust and a land of flies,
A land of sweat and burning eyes
Where the strong one lives and the weak one dies,
That's Africa to me.

But be it day or be it night,
Be it black or be it white,
Be it wrong or be it right:
It's paradise to me.

Geoff Hill

SINGING WITH THE RAIN

*Singing with the Rain is about Stafford Castle, a
three-mile walk from home, where a group of us
children used to go. No adults came with us. We used
to go out all day and return home at tea time.*

We scrambled over the crumbling walls
of castle ruins up on the hill,
slithered down the motte on bums,
frocks rucked up round our waists.
We picked ourselves up,
smoothed ourselves down,
set off for home

down Muddy Lane,
a rutted short-cut of muck
that sucked down sandals.
Blackberries in plenty for picking
told tales on our lips and hands.
Briars drew blood. Mud clung to our legs,
dyed socks and knees red.

Back on the road we sang at the top
of the scale as the rain pelted down,
beat a retreat on the drum.
We out-shouted the trumpet of thunder,
screamed with the forks of the flash,
clung to each other like treacle,
danced in the puddles and splashed.

A car stopped. *Want a lift?* We piled in,
Clambered into the back, packed
shoulder to shoulder, dripped into the seats,
made our mark on the doors, on the floor.
Stranger danger did not enter our heads,
nor thoughts of who he might be. Back then,
childhood was good. We sang.

Wendy Goulstone

A LETTER FROM HOME

The torture of a gruelling day,
And eyes too tired to see,
Were suddenly there no more
when a letter came for me.

The writing that I knew so well,
Words meant for me alone;
The war was gone and I was in
a world all of my own.

I read in silent happiness,
The news, line after line,
And sank and rose on clouds of joy
and lost all sense of time.

The words so tender washed clear
the aches of a blazing day,
And carried me, momentarily,
A thousand miles away.

Geoff Hill, January 1978
Age 21 (as a soldier)

ON THE WAY TO SCHOOL

A trip we take for granted
In weather hot and cool
Whether bus or shank's pony
The journey to your school

Bike or a scooter
Or a rolling hoop
Consider the crocodile
Or another kind of group

A schoolboy in Africa (Ukraine)
Has to navigate the signs
Along with vicious wildlife (soldiers)
He has to spot the mines

So let your son or daughter
Know how lucky they are
Beware of the dangers
Then they'll go far!

Paul Clark

THE BIRDS

Cwm Idwal, Snowdonia

Picture the scene.
A freezing day, no sun, low cloud.
An amphitheatre of black slate cliffs
glistens with ice, a backdrop of menace.
On the ledges, snow clings.
Blackened moss grips
and saps the drips.
A few sparse saplings
dig their roots into cracks
and struggle up the rocks.
A frozen pool lies centre stage,
shackles of ice clasp prisoners of reeds.
A barricade of boulders rings the pool,
tops capped with snow.
The heavy air is still, primeval, silent.

Enter stage left two muffled figures,
watching their step around the blocks
and chips of broken stone.
The desolate waste beckons.
Enchantment leads them in.
Entranced they gaze
upon the brooding walls.
They sense the spirit of the place
and want to leave,
but, led deeper in, select a spot,
brush off the snow and sit.

From his pack he takes a tin and opens it.
She finds a bag of bread, receives the tin,
begins to spread and passes back
a sandwich to the other one.
Hungry, they begin to munch.

And then a strangeness in the atmosphere,
a feeling that one gets, sometimes,
of being watched,
that staring eyes are fixed
in concentration on one's every move.

The tension builds.
A bird is perched some distance from their seat,
a seagull far from shore.
They see another,
and again one more.
Then six arrive
and join the semicircle by the pool.
Five more fly in and take their place
and still they come.
Some telepathic message draws them in.
They make no noise except
the flapping of their wings.
They watch and wait.

Closer they come.
The circle closes as the seagulls
edge towards their prey,
an imperceptible advance.
The couple sit stock still,
mouths motionless,
anticipate attack.
Nerves begin to crack.

I don't like this, I think we ought to go.
I can't help thinking of that Hitchcock film.
She, with a look of scorn, declares,
I said it was a bad idea
To bring sardines.

Wendy Goulstone

DOWN TO THE WATERFALL

Down to the waterfall
Twisting, winding
Closed in by the green and grey
Silver, and copper red
The light dims stage by stage
Step by slow step
Following the narrow track
That comes and goes away

Down to the waterfall
Vague hints of sound
Water rushing, clear and white
Foaming, to the dark pool
Sunlight catching high spray
Rainbow fragments
Drop through a secret dappled glade
On pollen laden air

Down to the waterfall
Peaceful escape
Stepping slowly into cold
Chilling knees, thighs, waist, chest
Swimming at peace at last
Frozen thoughts
Nothing now but the motion
Primeval comfort

EE Blythe

STAFF ROOM

Tattered papers droop sadly from the crowded noticeboard
- health and safety, child protection, Ofsted -
most ignored and unread,
en route to the wastepaper bin.
Dirty mugs cluster on the worktop next to the stale bread.
A solitary baked bean clings to the hot tap.
On the coffee table,
piled next to the union magazines,
an opened box of fondant cakes
proves attractive to a passing fly.
Later, desperate for a sugar rush,
a teacher will finish them off.
Dowdy chairs gather uncomfortably in small groups,
angled carefully to avoid the headteacher's gaze,
but within earshot of any nuggets of news.
Light filters in through vertical blinds
but somehow fails to fill the room.
The gloom is permanent and unforgiving.
The dishwasher gurgles,
desperate to be unloaded,
but it will have to wait.
It's time for lessons to begin.

John Howes

THE LEGEND OF ST BRIAVEL'S CASTLE

The Legend of St Briavel's Castle is based on a happening there, when a Youth Hostel Association warden, working late in the solar room, then her office, heard a baby crying in the room. Later, workmen repairing the ceiling over the fireplace found the skeleton of a baby. We have stayed there, now a youth hostel, and it is a very un-nerving place. The solar room is now the YHA sitting room. There are several ghost stories about the castle.

At dead of night you may hear the cry,
if you sit alone in the solar room,
you may hear the cry of a child concealed.
It howls within the castle walls
but you will not see the baby there.
Now hear the story that I was told.

The King owned the castle, I was told.
His hunting horn was heard to cry
throughout the deep Dean Forest there
that the queen could see from her solar room
within the castle's strong stone walls
where she sang to a child she had concealed,

her tiny love-child well concealed,
of which the King had not been told,
kept within the castle walls
where none could hear his hungry cry
in the Queen's own private solar room
by the warmth of the fire there.

But a fever spread in the village there
and took the baby she concealed.
He died in the Queen's own solar room
at dead of night, so I was told.
His mother could only sob and cry
when the king was out riding beyond the walls.

'I want to keep him within these walls,'
the mother sighed as she sat there.
The faithful maid began to cry,
'Madam, we'll keep your baby sealed,
to ward off evil, as I've been told,
in the chimney of your solar room.'

The maid and the Queen made a little room
high inside the chimney wall,
and the king and his followers never were told
of the secret child that was hidden there.
Centuries later, in the solar concealed,
a resident heard a baby cry.

Workmen in the solar room,
repairing the crumbling ceiling there,
high inside the chimney wall
found bones of a tiny child concealed.
And late at night, as I have told,
you, too, may hear a baby cry.

Wendy Goulstone

BRADGATE LOCKDOWN

Now empty and deserted lies the Park.
Age-riven oaks shake branches at the blast,
The racing rain and sky cloudfull of dark.
But, ripped away, the tender leaves fly fast.
Oblivious to weather, now the deer
Expand across the once-ways of our day
And nonchalantly graze, forgetting fear,
Where once in grass the hidden litter lay.
On warmer mornings comes the May birds' call.
No jolly voices braying through the haze.
No bikes, or prams or pushchairs on the ways,
Smooth vipers slide to sun-laze on the wall.
Was it like this when Nine-Days Jane rode there?
Just oaks, with deer and sky and open air.

Chris Rowe

MADRID AIRPORT, 2020

A giant packet of Twix Minis,
A man standing and talking with animation
into a telephone,
Oslo, Paris, Athens

Shiny, clean tiles,
An Easyjet plane slowly reversing onto
The scorched runway,
Singapore City, Brasilia, Wellington

Final call for the Aswan flight,
"Istanbul!" shouts a man
Pointing in front of the departure board,
Menorca, Philadelphia, Kiev.

Out there, it's 21 degrees.
Back home, it's only seven.
Birmingham beckons.

Back to reality.

John Howes

AT WORDSWORTH HOUSE

My hand on the bannister
where his lay   where he slid
down from bed to breakfast
porridge bowl   milk cup
before a quick run to school

prayers said   songs sung
tables chanted   letters scratched
with feather quill
and the run home again
to chase round flower beds
vegetable plots   hen pens
throwing windfall apples
in sibling battles then

a scramble over the garden wall
or a hushed creep below windows
and out of the gate to escape
in a mad dash to the river bank
to toss sticks   race with them
yell   mine won   and fall sprawling
on the grass in a tangle of arms and legs
laughter and high pitched screeches
reaching the ears of the town

until called in   hauled in to bed
up the stairs where my hand
now slides on the bannister.

Wendy Goulstone

THROW ME IN THE SEA

Throw me into the sea
I want to swim out
Take me West to the coast
I want to swim out

I've got my own best spot
If I could get there
Wide sandy open beach
If I could get there

We could play obstacle boule
Just like we used to
To dry off and warm up
Just like we used to

I dream I'm body surfing
Freedom in the waves
Watching dolphins enjoying
Freedom in the waves

Take me over to the coast
I want to swim away
Oh, throw me in the sea
I want to swim away

EE Blythe

DRAYCOTE

Which way this time? Clockwise or not?
Either way the wind cuts across the dam,
that mile-long slog.

Decision made, we pass the shop,
the yacht club and the wintering boats.
The rigging flaps.

By picnic bench a clutch of coots
in dinner suits and white bow-ties
peck at the grass. Mile one is done.

Along the straight, a glimpse of hall
and spires up on the hill. The tower
marks the turn and upward slope.

No little grebes today.
Mallards with last year's young
have grabbed their spot.

More sheltered now.
A few dried leaves cling to the trees.
The soil is sodden and the berries rot.

Mile two has passed. At halfway point
a weathered seat provides a break
and windswept view.

Three miles. A muddy patch
marks the spot where one can watch
the alpaca flock, a placid lot.

A new-laid path across the bog,
a smelly stretch when summer's hot,
now dark and dank.

Four miles. With cameras and binoculars
a pair of twitchers in the hide
watch the show.

Gulls glide in drifts. Geese prowl the shore.
Black-cloaked cormorants perch on broomsticks,
waiting their chance.

And last, the dam, the final sprint,
with muffled scarves round tingling ears
and thoughts of soup.

Wendy Goulstone

Highly commended in the Campaign to Protect
Rural England Poetry Competition 2010

YNYSMAENGWYN

*Ynysmaengwyn is the name of the house and estate
where John Corbett, who did a lot for Towyn (now
Tywyn), lived. We knew it as Corbett Mansions, and it
was in a bad state in the 1960s, but the garden and
derelict out-buildings were a paradise for children with
imaginations. It is now a camping and caravan park.*

Sunshine and moonbeams
Nests in the trees
Hiding in the honeysuckle
Picking green beans
Beating the blackbirds to ripe currants, black
Grub laden treasure from wild raspberry canes

Bats in the half light
Owls' unblinking eyes
White flowers glowing
Ghosts in the night
Running through damp grass, disturbing moths
Picking 'sticky grass' from hair, and old jumpers

Fallen blocks of stone
Overgrown walls
Dens, and secret hidey holes
Huge black insects
Snakes basking unblinking in the sun
Scratches, scrages, bites, and nettle rash

Wild and forgotten
The gardens of youth

EE Blythe

STORMY NIGHT IN CHESTER

It is a frost twig snapping night.
With howling gusts the wind hurls
Into the great nave of the church
Slamming the door behind us,
The silent safety of the ship
Enfolds us. And the service begins.
Jesus walking on the water is the theme.

Then the storm of the night tap-bangs
Against the windows, thrashing
And bruising the coloured glass.
The whole building heaves and rolls
In the blackness,
Lashing, splashing waves
In the wind, screaming in our ears.

Faintly through the groaning
Of the creaking boat boards
I can just hear him calling me.
'Take courage, it is I.
Put your feet on the water.
Feel the springy turf
Of the blue green surf.'

I struggle to clamber overboard.
'Yes Lord, I'm coming,' I cry.
But in my mind's fearful eye
I see that far country
Where this first step is leading.

I feel my feet sinking,
There is a hurried sound
Of splashing feet, the thudded impact
Of strong arms round me.
I am held tight.
Then once more
I'm in the safe hold of the ship.
We rise to sing the Nunc Dimittis.

Sylvia Mandeville

I'M IN YOUR HOUSE

I'm in your house.
You didn't leave the door open.
Locksmith,
I'm a locksmith
and thanks for the biscuits,
but only one nibble per visit.
Your neighbour's dog; it's not a challenge
thanks to some Valium and steak mix.
I go to her house sometimes and watch Dominic
Littlewood.
I remember to put the remote controls in the dog's
basket.
Gives her the creeps...delicious.

My favourite thing is to leave a tiny microphone
I listen to your confusion as you wonder where you
put your glasses or your keys.

Or I borrow a pair of pliers or scissors, bring them
back in a few days,
always remembering to leave them in the wrong
place.
Now I have a collection of nearly 100 comfy venues
where I can spend some me-time
But I don't do much damage...
just enough to get people worried.
One unpleasant time
a man with a gun...
I faked an accident.
Luckily his family were out and
coppers aren't like Columbo in real life you know

I especially like not having to spend any money on
heating or eating.
Time to move on soon.
But not before I relax in your house.
I just want to use your loo,
number two, sorry.
Might take the covers off your bed.
Did you do that when you went out this morning?
You'll be convinced you did.

Sometimes I bite your cheese straight out of the
packet.
I can't say what I do in your bath
but I will say I'm touched.
One unpleasant time
a chihuahua surprised me but enjoyed the steak
and then started choking. I couldn't do anything,
watched it die
which was sad.
I had to take the piece out with your crochet hook
and Ta Da!!!
it's natural causes
unless your vet is Quincy.

So now I'm looking through your photos,
I just take one or two
especially as you look so sensational
in your Sexy Sunday Best.
See you next week
and
you know where I'll be.
...
I'm in your house.

Chris Wright

KESWICK MARKET IN THE RAIN

Keswick market slopes and sloshes
from top to bottom of the town,
dripping its wares from stalls
heavy with hand-knit jumpers.
Subtle sheep-colours cut a dash
with cable twists, rich in age-old customs.

Jars of pickles, chutneys, honey, jam,
sweet-tongue strollers to come and buy.
They can't compete with the curry stall
with its come-and-eat-me-now temptation.
A stack of plastic plates beside a steaming pot
await the wet and hungry stroller.

There's a needle and thread industry here
in Christmas hangings, capacious stockings,
advent calendars with pockets in sizes to suit.
A stall-holder pokes a stick under the canopy,
releases a downpour that splashes passing legs
already too drenched to notice.

We finish the round, call it a day, splash back
up the hill to the comfort of self-catering cottage,
peel off soaked shoes, shake dripping brollies,
strip off sodden clothes, switch on the gas fire,
sink onto the sofa with a sigh and doze for a while,
wake with a craving for hot chocolate.

Wendy Goulstone

CITY NIGHT

Walking around with my hands in my pockets
Head down, shoulders hunched,
Daring the wind to blow in my face
Secretly hoping it will blow me away
Defying the rain to touch me
Quietly wishing it to soak me through
Not looking where I'm heading
Nowhere in mind to go

Reflection of lights in growing, gathering puddles
Dancing to the rhythm of the wind
Swirling and whirling the dead leaves along
Making boats on the miniature seas
Braving the towering wavelets
Sinking to the gravel sea-bed
Kicked aside by giants' feet
Not even seen
Like me

Cathedral bells ringing
A cantilena from the sky
For whom does the bell ring?
For me, but for why?

As I kick up dirty papers, and wander
Through the mud-strewn concrete concourse
And I watch the neon rainbows race
I can hear the nearby empty voices
Of the lost and lonely souls
Who are talking much too loud
Beer in their blood, false courage in their hearts
And a little scotch mist in their heads

But they don't notice me
They've no reason to see
I'm no-one
With nowhere to go

EE Blythe, 1976

WATCHING UNOBSERVED

A century ago,
This young man,
Would have been church bound,
With a wife in wizened worsted,
And children calico brown,
Kneeling in prayer,
On hard wooden benches.
Sure rendering unto Christ.

No central heating then.
No welfare state then.
No rejoicing at Clem's new
Jerusalem.

Today,
This young man,
Unblemished face,
How I wish this young face was mine.
His is smooth like Esau.

Mine is pock marked by self injury.
The hair line visibly receding.
And much more than this,
The teeth falling out.

He sits astride,
A colossus of a lorry,
Orange and yellow.
The name of a private company,
Not English.
On its side.

Detritus collecting,
That's the posh word for collecting poo.

Minions running to collect and discharge the bins,
With the fury of a lottery prize hunter,
How strange.
This energy.
And all on minimum wage.

And,
Yellow Jacket,
Flashing incandescent.
As he turns the wheel,

It's that briefest of moments,
When,
The sodium glare of street lights,
Dim,
And are met by the pale frail sunlight,
Of a cold November morning fighting its way through,
As I watch.
Un-observed.

And get this,
The sudden Breeze
Of arching Newspapers,
In the wind.

Splaying like Confetti.

I watch.
It's Sunday,
In Cheltenham.
I am this year's Santa.
In the Burlington Arcade.

Equity Member 41761.
Logging on for the early shift.

Simon Grenville

BLOWN BY THE WIND

Navigate dark water
Tumble white rapids
Catch on subterranean rocks
Negotiate intruding boulders
Drift in calm streams
Drop
Over unseen waterfalls

Pace quiet green footpaths
Step through cool woodlands
Scale sheer, high escarpments
Hike across boundless moorland
Walk sun-warmed sand
Fall
Over crumbling cliff edges

'Til it's known if Life or Death prevails
This will be the way it must be
We cannot control
We can only be
Blown by the wind

EE Blythe

ENCOUNTER AT WORDSWORTH HOUSE, COCKERMOUTH

Sitting under the tree in the hidden garden
I picked up an apple, a windfall among dozens,
round and rosy, too good to let rot.

'They are not good to eat, and there are worms,'
said a boy, six or seven years old, watching me
as I opened my mouth.
I smiled. He was wearing costume, a child,
perhaps, of the cook telling tales to visitors
by the wood-fired kitchen range.

'That hen there,' he said, 'that one is mine.
It likes to escape and peck the cabbages.
I like to wander free, too.
Have you seen the river over the wall?
It is full today after the rain. Sometimes
I walk with my sister along the bank.

'In springtime, marsh marigolds glow golden;
in summer, teasels grow tall in the reeds,
then it is time for blackberry tart.
In winter we fill sacks with glossy holly
for the house, the berries glistening.
In the firelight they glow like rubies.

'When I have learned all my letters I shall write
poems. I try and try. My tutor says, One day,
my boy, your name will travel wide.
Don't eat the apple, Miss.' But I can't resist a bite.
The bitterness brings tears. I close my eyes.
When I look up, he has gone.

Back in the house, the cook puts on her coat.
'I saw your son,' I say. 'You saw him, did you?
I've seen him, too. He is not mine.'

Wendy Goulstone

THE MAZE

In a maze I twist and turn
And still I find
No way to go
For sure

If I go away, will you
Come and see me
Just to make sure
I survive

There is a wall
High, black, and tall
And if I turn, I face
The Monster Of The Maze

Eyes stare, but do they see me
Hands reach, but will they catch me
And if they do, then will they kill me
And if I'm dead, what will I then see
The Monster Of The Maze

We all will come this way, some time
Yet only pass the threshold once
But at times we stand beside the Old Way
Caught in tight answers, locked to the Earth
With The Monster Of The Maze

And what will The Monster do?
And who is The Monster – Who?

And where is The Maze
And where be this world
All inside my mind

The rain falls
And the time ticks on
Sleep will not come to me

EE Blythe

MIST

Oh, it was so misty
that Friday night by the sea -
West Bay enveloped in a fog,
the waves unusually silent and listening.
We strolled amid the calm,
waiting expectantly for the roughness to return.

But the white gave way to the blue,
the sky filled with sun,
unadulterated and honest,
fresh as a new-born day.
And it shone into our troubled hearts.
The gulls took flight,
the boats set sail
and we were away,
Again.

John Howes

YNYS

Tumbling, rumbling, wind down the valley roars
Birds hitting the edge to make a stall turn
Sunlight glinting on rain-dripping leaves
And the smell of the sea in the air

Chugging, grumbling, the tractor comes to life
Rolling and turning those huge 'cotton reels'
The crack of plastic from the wrapping machine
And the scent of the hay in the field

Ticking, clicking, crickets sound in the sun
Grass sways as, unseen, basking snakes move
The evening squabble begins in the rookery
And the aroma of food on the breeze

Bubbling, burbling, the estuary sand goes
The wide water reflects the village lights
Night noises take over – nightjar and owl
And the sounds of fun from the pub

EE Blythe

Press Pause

PASSIONS

DO YOU STILL LOVE ME?

Do you still love me
after all these years?
Or is it just familiarity now?
I do love you,
not with the passion of our youth,
but for always, and sometimes
with affection that creeps up on me.

But you, how do you feel?
It's been such a long time together.
I know you need me around
and are lonely when I am not around.
But love –
is there still love?

I need you now I am old and arthritic.
You are strong and can reach things and undo jars
and mend things,
and I rely on you.
But is that love, or need, I wonder?
We are of the generation of men
being strong and silent,
showing no emotion.
Softness was not allowed.
You cover yours by going in your man-cave shed with
beer and music:
you love to remember
and to cry.

Ruth Hughes

LOVE IS GREAT,
EXCEPT WHEN IT ISN'T

Years ago, I was in the south-east
and an old college friend kindly agreed
to give me a lift to Euston station.
When we arrived, I asked if she deserved a kiss.
She said, "Yes," so I kissed her once on the cheek.
Mistake.
Big mistake.

The following day I was thinking of her all the time.
I think it must be what being in love feels like, but...
I'm sure being in love is great when you know
that the other person feels the same way about you,
but when your own feelings are doing things
you would rather they didn't, it's annoying.

It's more than annoying.
It's a feeling of not being in control.
The feelings lasted for three days.
I still remember the episode with a shudder.

Some psychologists say that
people fall in love because they kiss,
not the other way round.
I think they have a point.

Jim Hicks

SCHOOL PRESENTATION DAY

They know how not to put on a show.
No images, no music, no performances;
just a table covered by piles of certificates,
a single chair for the headteacher.
Students, now adults, drift in embarrassed;
Hushed expectancy is not rewarded.
Only the dull drone of alphabetical names.
Applause ripples and runs out,
Proud parents shift position in stiff chairs,
The clock ticks on unremarkably.

And yet, my son,
My son,
gets top student in psychology.
And nothing else matters
Except his glorious, emphatic smile
Which says
I have turned it all around,
I have scaled this mountain,
I stand at the summit
And I can see
The other side.

John Howes

MOTHER'S DAY

Oceans of taffeta, rustling, crackling, hissing and
sissing
Galaxies of netting, foaming, rising, floating and
crunching
Scratchy lace, breath-stopping boning
Chattering beading, breath-stealing lacing
And over it all, a mother's beady eye
Always a mother
The bride's mother
Insisting on sticking to rules
Ruling the roost

As if it was her day, not her daughter's
Whose joy, three hours before, is now in shreds
Meringue after shift, pom-pom after fur
Meringue, meringue, meringue
It rather takes the edge off the pleasure
It rather destroys the girlish delight
Of finding THE dress, the one
For that special day, to entrance The One

Make it stop. Now!

Defeated, dejected, trailing behind
Blank eyed, set mouthed, dragging her feet
Not happy with the final choice
The mother's choice
Mother's paying!

Plans for eloping, a Registry wedding
In a far off town, or country
These grow and die in her distressed mind
All the romance planned out of the day
Planned to the Nth degree

So not real, not true, not their day
Not until they can get away!!

EE Blythe

HOMECOMING

Yes, I'm down on my luck.

I've done a lot of things I shouldn't do,
and spent too much money doing them.
I'm hoping for a job. Any job.
The last job I had was looking after some pigs
and the pigs were better fed than I was.

I don't expect much from my father, after the way I
behaved. But at least I hope to have somewhere to
sleep,
something to eat and a lot of hard work.

What will I say to my mother?
She always wanted a grandchild.
How do I tell her she probably has a grandchild
but I don't know where or who?

Then there's Jake, my brother.
Our relationship was always...awkward,
especially when I left.
Perhaps he'll be put in charge of me.
That would be difficult, but hey, it's a living.

Round the hill, there's the farm, and there's my father.
Well, he seems pleased to see me.
At least that's something.

Jim Hicks

I MISS YOU

I don't miss the bad days and the wild look in your
eyes
I don't miss you standing there, spouting your lies
I don't miss those last years when you went so wrong
I don't miss the venom that came from your tongue

But

I miss you when there's something good to share
When I turn to speak and you're not there
I miss the weight of your presence in bed
The emptiness ahead fills me with dread

I miss all the music, the laughter, the fun
Life is so desolate now, on my own
I miss you with every living part of me
I miss the life together we planned, that now will
never be

But

I don't miss the bad days and the wild look in your
eyes

EE Blythe

CHECKMATE

Have you ever been afraid to say how you really feel?
Have you ever had a flood of words, but not known
which ones are real?
Like a game you play and play, hoping you will win
Each step you take, each move you make, seeps
further down within.

If your heart is like a chessboard, then the King is at
the core.
To get there is a battle, fighting all those Pawns.
The Rook is like the padlock, the question's where's
the key?
The answer must be simple, as there's only you and
me.

It's a tactical game, to win that King, to get that
craved checkmate.
Some people use their heads, others rely on fate.
With my Bishop, Queen and Knight, my King is truly
hidden.
But with the way you make your moves, nothing is
forbidden.

The flood of words starts to clear as the game is
always played.
With just two people, there's not much time before
each move is made.
But who will win this head to head, and will the King
be caught?
It doesn't matter either way, the enjoyment's in how
it's fought.

Lindsay Woodward

A FIREPACE

This is a poetic recounting of an actual incident. I was at a party getting some private peace time when a couple came into the room. The male went straight to the fireplace and began 'gushing' about it.

'Oh, it is, it is,
It's a Mackintosh, Daahhling
A Charles Rennie Mackintosh
Don't you see?
My God, it's so beautiful
Don't you see?
The lines,
The forms
The shapes
And the colour.
The bright cleanliness
So distinctive.
Don't you see?
Oh my God, it is sooo exquisite, Daahhling
A quintessential beauty.
I just want to touch it, caress it.
I want to feel its beauty in my soul, Daahhling
Don't you see?'

She thinks.......

'It's a bloody fireplace, Darling!
Just a pretty fireplace.
That's what I see.
I wish you would use that kind of language when you
look at me.
What about
My lines

My form
My shape
My colour?
I am bright
I am clean
And I am quite distinctive in my way.
Look at me!
Don't you see?
I am here, next to you, my darling
Why can't you see my quintessential beauty?
Look at me.
I want you to touch me, caress me.
Feel my beauty in your soul.'

She smiles and takes his arm and says

'Yes, it's lovely, isn't it darling?
Beautiful, I think.
Shall we go back to the party now?
I need another drink!'

Linda Slate

NO RHYMES FOR CHRISTMAS

A poem about Father Christmas?
No chance, said she,
To show it.

There are no rhymes for Christmas,
She said,
As a poet.
But I thought:
-as the years just whizz past,
Perhaps she doesn't know it.

But I loved her
and I could clearly see
That just to make the fizz last,
Perhaps I'd just agree.

So to live in lover's bliss wi't lass,
Yes yes, yes yes, says me.

Philip Gregge

NIGHTWALKER

Parkland stroll; the moon thrills a cloud.
A path, a pool apart from the crowd
You still your noisy mind
Miraculously alone,
Till the nearby factory's groan
Brings you back to the grind.
(by Lehrling)

Chris Wright

A POET'S LAMENT

I asked a lady where I work
To come around for tea
On Sunday afternoon, and we'd
recite some poetry.

With a wink she told me,
The voice a trifle mellow,
That I could view her Ruskin,
If I showed her my Longfellow.

And sure enough at 3 o'Clock,
She came with all her books,
But as I rubbed my hands with glee,
I think she read my looks.

After tea I made a start
With Chaucer's bawdy rhymes,
But she thought Maya Angelo
More suited to our times.

Perhaps with these poetic types
I just don't know my onions,
She left at four and to this day
I've still not seen her Bunyans.

Geoff Hill

THREE POSSIBILITIES

Once upon a time there were three possibilities.
Three possibilities with a future of infinite pathways.
Ethereal energies flitting through our realities,
Conjured by hopes and wishful thinking.
Barely touching,
But no less real in their presence.
A lifetime of giggles and tears, achievements and
failures,
And crises.
A lifetime of mixed joys and sorrows,
Innocence, innocent play, and in time,
Adult responsibilities.
A lifetime never realised.
Robin, Rhiannon, and Cornelius.
Which one were you?
Which one would you have been?

EE Blythe

JUST GO
(COMMUNICATION 1)

Oh go. Please go.
I love you, but there's a limit !
I want a bit of Me time (Is that selfish ?)
I need a bit of peace.

Oh go. Please go.
Don't take a breath, and start again.
My ears are switching off (My brain already has)
I need a bit of quiet.

Oh go. Please go.
There's such a thing as too much.
We reached that a while back (I feel trapped)
I need to be alone.

Oh go. Please go.
But please come back soon.

(Why did I just say that?)

EE Blythe

THE PHONE RINGS (COMMUNICATION 2)

The phone rings again
and I know who it will be
I'm an almost housebound audience
a listening ear, you see

I cannot stop the torrent
of excited verbosity
It doesn't matter anyway
he doesn't want to hear me

So I listen, without a word
say Mmm and Aah occasionally
And close my ears as best I can
while he talks on incessantly

And when the need to tell it all
has finally ceased to be
He says goodbye, and that is that
and blessed silence falls on me

EE Blythe

EDINBURGH FESTIVAL

That dress,
That loose fitting muslin dress,
Blue white virgin serge.

That dress,
That one that hung over ,
Rather than clutched your body,
The one that I caressed ,
With such freedom.

That dress,
With
The bright white whale bone buttons,
Carelessly tied,
That dress.
Carelessly hanging from the rehearsal room door.
That dress.

Simon Grenville

BIG MATCH REPORT

Wedding guests, tune up in the posh
part of the park; happy snapping they
celebrate, bride and Sun radiate. All
wearing grey and black and white
and counterpointed by Jersey lilies and
busy lizzies and chrysanthemums
with a coda of laurels and cedars.
Bridesmaids are land girl ruddy; sky
blue dresses overblown with enough
folds to hide a zeppelin. Their uncle
scowls at the nosey onlooker in the
Wasps rugby shirt.
The horsey bride and Piggott-faced
groom still seem ideal stable mates,
corralled by flowerbeds. Her white
dress shows, not virginity, not a
mourning white for a lost single life
but a promise to pursue
perfection beginning this day. The
indecisive warm air currents meander,
bringing the bride's "Poison" perfume
into competition with the
honeysuckle.
A small boy, Xerox of the adults in
top hat and tails, is now distracted
by a rolling tennis ball. He has to
aeroplane both arms for balance
while Collymore kicking the lime.
Soon they leave the park, re-grouped
and renewed. Later the Tribune will
freeze them forever in a picture next to
the usual bad news.   **Chris Wright**

ODE TO THE SAS

Fight on fight on brave soldiers,
Through dirt and pain and sweat,
The campaign may be long and slow,
But you will get there yet.

Keep faith, keep faith brave soldiers
In the things you believe are true
And never submit to the slime and grit
That's always threatening you.

Strike on, strike on, brave soldiers
For we know you are right
And take with you a prayer or two
We send to you tonight.

And perhaps, perhaps, brave soldiers
In times of time to come,
Peace will reign on us again
Through the things that you have done.

Geoff Hill

PLANET

ONCE UPON A TIME

Once upon a time,
The sun shone the whole summer
Once upon a time,
It snowed every single winter
Once upon a time,
Milk came in glass bottles and was delivered to your
door
Once upon a time,
Bread was baked in the village bakery – and was
delivered to your door
Once upon a time,
Petrol was under a pound – per gallon
Once upon a time,
We spent shillings and pence, and measured
imperially
Once upon a time
You could get educated without getting into debt
Once upon a time,
People with ordinary jobs could afford to buy houses
Once upon a time,
People got married before they had children
Once upon a time,
Mummy stayed at home while Daddy went out to
work
Once upon a time,
Women couldn't vote
Once upon a time,
Smog choked our cities and towns
Once upon a time,
Fifty out of every thousand children died before their
first birthday

Once upon a time,
Britannia ruled the waves – and owned the most
slaves
Once upon a time...
They were the good old days, right?

Steve Redshaw

FORAGER'S DILEMMA

Is it a mushroom or is it not
Put me in a coffin or add it to the pot
Will it complement my sage and thyme
Or will I lose the plot

Fungi has many uses
To fly in astral signs
In South America
Check out the Nascar lines

Many years in Baldock
I purchased mushroom mulch
I had a few bags over
And picked buttons for my lunch

Ever heard of lichen
Algal and fungal team
Indicating clean air
No, not a dream

All legumes are useful
That's beans and beans
Nitrogen in nodules
Make sure you tell the we'ans

I could carry on extolling
Virtues of fungal fruits
But be careful before you eat them
Don't meet the men in suits

Paul Clark

FIRST DAY OF SPRING

I could feel spring coming a good few weeks ago.
I could smell it, hear it in the urgency of the bird song,
also the nights were drawing out
I notice this because I have hens at the bottom of my
garden and I shut them up when it goes dark.
Now we have passed the official first day of spring.
I love the sound of all the birds singing;
I thought they sang from joy as I do
but I learned from a nature programme
that they have to sing to entice a mate,
also to protect their territory.
I was disappointed.
I thought that God had made them sing for our
pleasure
but no.

As I go for my daily walk down to the crossroads and
back,
I appreciate all the appearing spring flowers growing
now -
primroses, cowslips, violets, celandines.
The wild cherry is covered with white blossom.
The hedges are beginning to shoot green now.
I can almost see changes each day.

Then there are swathes of daffodils
that groups of villagers have planted over the years.
I am told there is plenty of frog spawn
down the Great Central Way too.

Ruth Hughes

THE LAST ONE TREE

Remember my primal forest and Eve
Children danced round us, our catkins descended
couples making love under or on every bough
you always needed something to believe
Science fiction warnings have ended
You just read romances now

I spread my canopy a mile wide
Life sheltered from the dwindling glare
late flowers for the butterfly and bee
I reach two miles into sky of grey sulphide
My swirling seeds strewn to the callous air
I must go to make way for HS43

you slew the Thunnor Oak for your new deity
defamed the worshippers on the heath
Now destruction thunders to new ends
In the Museum to be a sliced curiosity
After 300 years death is a relief
You can get away faster to see friends

"That big cake you're standing on
Will endure forever" have sworn
The Economists, and Priests make devotion
name more animals now gone
Then in a wailful choir the small gnats mourn
Your back garden, replaced by ocean.

Chris Wright

A WALK IN LOCKDOWN

Enjoy the glories, wandering to giddy heights.
Daily exercise is the order of the day.
An hour plus, every morning
When will it end? Will it end?

I love it. The daily walking.
Time to think. Memories of childhood walks.
Amongst wildflowers, red campion, foxgloves.
Off I traipse. What's the weather?
Wet. A rainproof jacket is required.
Rough, blustery winds destroy umbrellas.

I love it. The daily walking.
Shoes sturdy prepared for puddles, wet grass.
I'm desperate to escape. They come too close.
Will the dog walkers, families, runners, couples,
Move? Respect should be observed at all times. Is it?
I love it. The daily walking.
Be kind and distance, two metres, no less.
They must all distance. Why don't they care?
I'm fearful. I must catch the virus.
When will it end? The longed-for grandchildren's
cuddles.
Grandchildren's weekly tea-time visits to return. I miss
them.

I love it. The daily walking.
People – girls, boys, ladies, men, maybe with dogs.
Dogs, sometimes three, large and hairy.
Two small and yappy, snarly at my feet.
One pretty, exquisitely well-behaved specimen.
I really love dogs, at a distance, in Lockdown.

I love it. The daily walking.
Another morning sunny, hot, fierce sun,
Open-toed, sequined sandals, inappropriate for
walking.
A floppy wide-brimmed hat is worn and protective
sun lotion.
The burning hot sun pierces my freckles.

I love it. The daily walking.
Do I really want to brave the hordes?
To move away when nobody notices me?
Don't they realise I might have the virus?
I'm strolling away, up the lush green, grassy hill.
Why don't you people move away from me?

I love it. The daily walking.
That young man thoughtfully crossed the road.
I want to praise him for his consideration. He is kind.
Faith returns to my heart. A lovely smiling fella.
Success, at last, I stand on top of the hill.
Views for miles across lush green meadows.

I love it. The daily walking
It's quiet. Listen. Sunday.
No rumble of vehicles on the distant motorway.
Only birds twittering, blackbirds, sparrows.
Hark, a bright red-breasted robin tut-tutting.
Owning a perch on the highest, tallest TV aerial.

I love it. The daily walking.
Nobody around. I am accustomed to a lonesome walk.
Do I mind? Not anymore. I love my own company.
Tall trees overhang pathways, cows moo in distant fields.
A daily habit, quiet walks, getting to know myself.
What about the future?

I love it. The daily walking.
I won't rush round, browsing, shopping.
A revelation. I enjoy my own company.
In the future, there will be more time to think.
It's great to ruminate on issues, family, friends, global.
Knowledge – there are two sides to each problem.
Be kind, listen to problems, and help people.
I love it. My daily walking.

Kate A.Harris

WE DID NOT LISTEN

We cannot say we did not know
Voices spoke of it long ago
And as the span of time decreased
The voices' urgency increased

So now, on the point of No Return
Where the land will flood, and the sky will burn
We have to act decisively
Convincing those who speak derisively

That the danger is real and happening now
Up in the heavens as it is down below
The signpost is showing the distance is small
The empire of the humans is heading for a fall

For our children, and our children's children's sake
There are steps now we all must take
It's down to you, and it's down to me
Because there is no planet B

EE Blythe

LOCKDOWN

I saved another life again today –
My fourth to date, beginning start of May.
From certain floating death I've now set free
Three beetles and, in warmer times, a bee.

But then, I've slaughtered one more slimy slug
I scooped up in the garden as I dug,
And snails I've exiled to the wheelie bin
For Transportation later for their sin.

For something just to do I stare and sigh.
The blackberries are past their picking date,
To stave off boredom, though, it's worth a try.
To plant more runner beans is far too late,
So I decide to clean and paint the gate
And then tomorrow I could watch it dry.

Chris Rowe

AND THEN I DID SOMETHING STUPID

(Or if only my grandson hadn't broken his ankle at an inopportune time)

I was late cutting back the buddleia
It's not the sort you can just hack down
The flowers are not pink or lilac spikes
They're orange, and they're round

Armed with secateurs, and sharp pruning saw
I dragged the step-ladder out the door
And sinking its feet firmly into the clay
Climbed up, and happily began pruning away

But the buddleia snatched at my hair, and held tight
The only solution was to cut the branch free
And that's when, quite suddenly, I took flight
As I'd shifted my centre of gravity

I flew through the air, with an intake of breath
Thinking "This is it. This is death"
On the old strawberry trough I unfortunately landed
And like an upturned tortoise was inevitably stranded

(LONG PAUSE and BREATHE)

I couldn't move, and there was no-one around
To see me lying, stunned, flat out on the ground
'Til a voice said "Hello" and "Are you OK?"
"I didn't think you'd be sunbathing today!"

She had a bad back, and I have bad knees
But somehow we managed to get me upright
We laughed like mad fools, as we checked all we
could see
And discovered, by some miracle, that I was actually
all right

I said "Thank You", and my friend set off again
But now my cuts and bruises were giving me some
pain
So I picked up my tools, and was then shocked to see
That the pruning saw had been lying underneath me

With only a minimum air of regret, I said
"No more gardening today, for me"
And having escaped with minimum damage
Limped in, and reached for the TCP

EE Blythe

WALKING BY ANOTHER BUILDING SITE

Destruction, green, green fields ripped up, hedges
grubbed out
Green issues, what green issues?
Our local fields gone, hedges gone and wildlife
The whole shebang. Nothing could be done.
Nobody listened, a done deal,
Not construction, destruction vehicles, done their
worst.

Today a long heavy goods lorry, stuck in mud.
The new estate's narrow road, too sharp corners.
Didn't watch its removal. Carried on walking.
A few minutes later off track, muddy footpath
Past overgrown ponds, undergrowth, natural, wildlife.

Before a building site and hundred new homes,
There were birds, a mixed flock of greenfinches,
Blue tits, sparrows, flitting by too quick to identify.
They lost their home to houses, removed, no birds.
Magpies took flight, no more. Gone.

I miss the green fields, hedges, birds, gone for ever.
Replaced with plastic chimney pots, just for show,
No smoke bellowing forth, that's a plus.
Fibreglass gables, all in one piece, lined up
Piles of red bricks, all the same, thousands in rows.

Heavy goods vehicles, diggers, front loaders full of...
What are they full of? Top soil for new gardens.
Told 'Great soil for 'posher' houses.' Are they built?
Are all the houses low cost? What is low cost?
Shared ownership homes, buy direct.

I've watched houses built, terraced, semis and
detached.
Who's planning to live there? Locals, refugees,
immigrants?
'Houses needed,' they say. Can we build enough?
Many more houses needed. Where shall they build
them?
Too many people and too few homes.

Everybody needs a home, yes, that's a fact.
Great new school to be built for new children?
More people, more traffic.
'Houses built towards villages, to the motorway,'
I'm told. 'A green belt,' I'm told.

Another says 'Green belt, just a narrow strip of land.'
'Next to the old railway track?' I ask,
Terrified of the answer. 'Only a narrow strip,'
I'm told. Unbelievable. 'Don't fell trees,'
We're told. 'Plant trees,' we're told.

'Keep trees, a green, clean environment,' we're told.
'Grow grass and flowers,' we're told.
What do I see? I see destruction of green grass,
Trees taken out, and hedges once teeming with
wildlife.
All gone, never to return. Disappointing to witness on
walks.

'A child's playground on the site,' I'm told.
'Where will it be?' I ponder.
'Will children play there, naturally children need to play?
Cars, will there be too many cars, vehicles,
Four by fours everywhere? Pollution.'
Planners: 'Do we really need more homes in our town?'

Kate A.Harris

EAGLE

(For Mary Oliver)

The mysterious Eagle adorns the great dome
I am impressed by avian majesty
As Tom and I invade his mountain home
binoculars reveal reality.

Magnificent wings command the air
I see every barb and vane
details are clear
No rabbit eludes a gaze so quick
beak to evoke fear
Prey must be consumed alive
Claws hold a pigeon chick
Desecrates my mind so naive

Indolently looking with a child's eye
knees tremble at the greatest mystery yet
We think we know the grand sky
We're looking at our own silhouette

Chris Wright

THE OWLS

A sonnet

The sun lies low on this December day.
Long shadows clutch our ankles as we move.
Ahead of us is golden tussocked grass
With gingery, dead dock and shining scrub.
Squat bushes mark the margin of a ditch.
Our glasses draw towards us distant sights:
A pale-edged face and staring orange eyes.
The short-eared owls are searching for their food.
Ash-grey and tawny masterful long wings
Display the hunters' power in the air,
The languid flapping and the swerving turn.
Tall sentinels of gilded sedge stand proud
But powerless to warn oblivious prey,
The voles that rummage through the well-known roots,
Unheeding victims of the floating death
That hovers unsuspected overhead.
The sun departs and leaves its farewell gift -
This golden peaceful scene before our eyes
Where one thing lives because another dies.

Chris Rowe

THE BATTLE OF BERT AND THE BIRDS

Old Bertram Watts detested birds
upon his garden plot. Every year they ate his peas,
and other stuff, but stealing cherries, that was worse
When they were ripe they took the lot, despite his
pleas.

He bashed a saucepan, jumped about and fired a
gun,
to no avail. It made the local babies wail. He swore.
His wife refused to cook his meals with all that din.
He blew a trumpet, bought red flags, did semaphore,

performed a war dance, lit bangers, ran around all
day.
The birds all came to watch the show, took a seat
with cousins, aunts. Bert feared the birds were there
to stay.
He cried, he wailed, he even wept. He stamped his
feet

and rolled in mud. Bitter tears ran down his cheeks.
He ran outside in tempest, snow, and tore his hair.
His wife left home, Bert did not have a bath for
weeks.
His clothes were filthy. He had nothing left to wear.

But the cherries were just turning ripe. Tomorrow I will
pick,
thought Bert. He phoned his wife, Come home for
cherry pie.
So back she came, washed his garments double
quick,
hung them on the line to dry all night. Bert wore just a
tie.

Next morning Bert woke with a shock. The cherries
all had gone.
In their place, from every branch, hung Bertram's
socks,
vests, trousers, shirts and jumpers, pants,
pyjamas, every one
too high for Bert to reach. And every bird, mole,
rabbit, fox,

with tweet, caw, chirp, hoot, screech, bark, growl,
sang, Bertram and all humans, heed us.
Take care of every wren, thrush, owl,
fish, flower, insect, tree, beast, fowl,
or you'll find out how much you need us.

Wendy Goulstone

WORLD

I give you cattle that graze
You give me fast food restaurants.
I give you crops of sugar
You give me piles of sweet-wrappers.

I give you valleys of green
You give me polluting motorways.
I give you friends and families
You give me half-a-mile car journeys.

I give you hills and mountains
You give me ski resorts.
I give you exotic islands
You give me charter holiday flights.

I give you birds that sing
You give me the shooting season.
I give you two legs to walk
You give me four wheels to drive.

I give you the need to survive
You give me the obsession of greed.
I give you all that you need
You give me all that I don't.

I give you a world that will last forever
You give me a sentence of death.

John Howes

ONE LITTLE MAN

One little man
Just because he can
Destroys the lives of others
Illegal bombs
Creating new tombs
For the bodies of our brothers

One little man
With a Napoleon complex
To stand astride all the land
For good or ill
Exerting his will
Over all that he can command

One little man
With a twisted view
Of a kingdom within his possession
Brings death and pain
And cruel loss again
Solely to feed his obsession

One little man
Just because he can
Throws the world into War

EE Blythe

THE RELEASE

He was released yesterday, early.
We were not expecting it to be so soon.
There was no one there to greet him
When we did meet up
His suit was limp and crumpled
Just taken from a long packed suitcase.
Slowly the fresh air and gentle breezes
Eased the creases
From the soft velvet
Glowing in the sunlight.
Rich cream and orange brown
Vibrantly patterned.
Back in July the day he went inside
He'd been wearing hairy tweed:
'Woolly Bear' we'd called him.
Today, well tailored
He edged up the stem from his cocoon
And flew away.

Sylvia Mandeville

INUNDATION

Cove, creek, cataract, bog
Foam, and floe, fountain and fog
Spume, spindrift, swamp and stream
Dew and damp, leak, sea, and steam
Sleet and storm, paddy field, puddle and pond,
Waterspout, whirlpool, loch and froth
Bubble, brook, bore, beck, burn and bay
Tempest, torrent, 'berg, blizzard and spray,
Waterfall, well, wave, ripple and channel,
Tsunami, mist, cloud and current, cascade and canal,
River, rip-tide, rapids, moat and humidity
Spurt, surge, icicle, splosh and liquidity,
Glacier, lagoon, leet and levada,
Downfall, passage, sound, swell and harbour
Deeps and delta, ditch and tide
Shallows and shower, tarn, trench and ice,
Bight and basin, reservoir, rain
Firth and fjord, ocean, gulf, maelstrom and main,
Source, slush, snow, lake, and hail
Trench and tide, marsh, mere and gale
Trickle and dribble
Water
Wet,
Drip

drip

Drop.
Splash!

Chris Rowe

134

HUGGING THE TREES

Coombe Abbey, November 2021

We all need a hug
said the notice
Hug a tree.
So we spread our arms
put our ears to the trunk
listened to the sap
pumping in its heart.

Sequoia gigantea
a gathering of kings
solemn for council
on the old hall lawn.
We, their subjects
looked up to them in awe
bowed our heads
and hugged them all
while grey squirrels scratched
in the autumn carpet
on the throne room floor.

Cones curled in our palms
glossy as chocolate
I planned a forest
imagined giants
searched for seeds
in the secret dark.
Nothing.
The squirrels had other ideas.

Wendy Goulstone

THE PAINTING

The painting looked like it was melting,
but it was the waterfall.
The water was moving.
Actually moving.
The overhanging leaves were rustling quietly
in the breeze created by the vertiginous fall
of the white water.
White water that flowed and dropped,
disappearing when it touched the dark pool
in the sheltered, secret glade.
A place outside of time,
a place outside of reality.
A step, a gateway, a door to another world.
A world that had no pressure
of continuous background noise,
no pressure of unrealistic expectations;
a place of peace, a place to rest.
To step into that place and leave
the dirty, artificial, plastic world of everyday.
To lie in the cold water,
beneath the patterns created by the trees.
To be lost in the patterns.
The changing patterns.
The hypnotic patterns.
And to never leave the painting.

EE Blythe

APOCALYPSE

The usual walk to the newspaper vendors
Sunday sees me strapped for cash
All the Observers turned to cinders
Writhing under the rain of ash
Warming cracks the azure dome
The newspaper headline reads DOOM!
My terminal fear is the familiar home
and your empty room

Professor Attenborough says
the Asteroid will strike Loughborough,
Professor John Cole says
it's created a black hole,
Professor. Jeff Hurst says keep calm; -
until the gamma ray burst.

Berlin landlocked and occupied
The planets wander off their ellipse
Tea Leoni's last reel suicide
My sun has already been eclipsed
You remember love on the beach
I imagined dolphins and saw Proteus
Just outside Poseidon's reach
No world, just the two of us
Headlong rush with no brakes
An adventure far from the last wave

Void. Now he sends earthquakes
And I can't be bothered even to shave
Martians, Brexit or Covid
Why the world's ending , I don't know
Apocalypse, dust and the thing I did:-
When you left, I watched through the kitchen window

Chris Wright

LIMERICK

O why do I look so absurd?
A puffin's a comical bird:
I'll never look sweet
With bright orange feet,
A clown-faced, sad-eyed, tubby nerd.

Chris Rowe

APPLES

They sat on the windowsill of our holiday home -
Saturn,
Rubinette,
King's Acre Pippin,
Adams Pearmain,
Kidds Orange,
Belle de Boscop,
Crispin and
Jonagold.
Each perfect in their imperfections,
Some deep purple, others nature green,
Fruits of the earth.
Rough-shaped, proudly inviting to the touch.

The old apple-seller set up his stall at Southwold
Market.
My love had chosen each by hand.
That one, please. And one of those.
And that's unusual - one of those too, please.
He told her a story about each one,
Like they were old friends being passed on
From his orchard to her shopping bag,
From his life to ours.

What beauty there was in her choosing,
What exquisite delight in her pleasure
At nine apples to enjoy,
A different taste each day,
Another chance to marvel at nature
Another chance to sweeten our life together.

John Howes

SPOT THE FONTS!

Is it a will or a want
When you have to deal with a font
Does it make you scowl or smile
Like an inscrutable crocodile

What meanings do you want to share
To be shy or perhaps to dare
You're definitely not a mouse
When you use zany Bauhaus

If you wish to travel far
How about using courier
Was that a hoof at the door
Don't worry it's a friendly centaur

If the press is cool it's not too late
How about using copperplate
Don't discard or throw away
Why not use trebuchet?

Have you met Franklin and Miriam?
I'm pretty cool with both of them
With many helpers I'm good to go
In my box I've minion pro

Helvetica or calibri
You could dine with me
With a pair of Singapore slings
But please, no wingdings!

Paul Clark

ANOTHER LOVELY THUNDERSTORM

Another lovely thunderstorm
Plus torrential rain
Neighbours closing windows
And shutting doors again

But if I lived in a forest
Or better, in the wilds
I'd be dancing naked
Jumping puddles like a child

I'd happily live on the road
If I could carry the gear
Waking with the sunrise
Follow the flow of the year

Lying beneath the night sky
The turning of the stars
The dark-time secrecy
Before the morning starts

Another lovely thunderstorm
And so my spirit soars
Oh to be one with nature
And not be trapped indoors

EE Blythe

SILENCE IN THE SNOW

The world is white and, deeply green,
Norwegian trees stand sentinel downhill
And slope headlong away. On sticks I lean,
My chosen route, a well-remembered thrill.
Enticing undulations lie in store,
A track of little hiccoughs in the snow,
When swift descents will speed me upwards more;
Jack-hammering the legs is how to go.
Just one decisive thrust and off I rush.
The tingling wind slaps stinging past my face.
Now comes that tricky corner, ice and slush,
With relish test my skill, then on I race.
Last, by that snow-heaped tree, a troll-like mound,
I brake. And savour silence all around.

Chris Rowe

LISTEN

Thwink, Thwink, Thwink, non-resounding surface

Ching, Ching, a chime

Tse Tse, Tse Tse, Tse Tse, gently underlining

Trren, Trren, Trren, Trren, Trren

Sound builds. Rhythms.
Regular and broken. Rising and falling. Waxing and waning.

Naked, feel the air all around.

Sensations run over skin, in snaking trails of iciness.

Rain. It is raining. Hear it.

The rain is the drummer. The garden is the drum kit.

EE Blythe

THIS USED TO BE A VERY NICE AREA

This used to be a very nice area:
We had good neighbours
The children had space
For growing up. We felt safe.

Until those screaming hoodlums arrived
Thugging around in their black leathers.
Shouting the odds late into the night
Showing off their superior horsepower.

It is difficult to avoid confrontations.
Somehow we must teach the kids
New strategies. Improve our own social skills.
We housemartins prefer the quiet life
And these swifts are almost too much to bear.

Sylvia Mandeville

PETS

THE CATS I HAVE WORKED FOR

I have worked for three cats.
Toby was a factory cat.
Susie was a theatrical cat.
And Caesar was a South London crime boss.
As black as your hat, with two white paws,
Toby's full name was Two-shoes Treaddell.
He began life catching mice, progressed to rats,
After which, he was made to wear a bell.
A hunter, Toby loved the woods.
He caught a rabbit once.
He didn't hurt it but brought it home as a gift.
He didn't understand why he got short shrift.
Susie Kit-Kat had a lovely nature.
A delicately painted tortoiseshell.
Her coat was soft and brown,
with a black, red and orange mix.
A well-travelled cat,
she accompanied me when I worked in Rep.
Food, a litter tray and me
Was all Susie needed to be happy.
Caesar, a handsome British Blue
had been used as a breeder.
Thrown out when he had leukaemia,
He lived by his wits and the need,
to survive.
He brought me a fillet steak.
My neighbour's dinner dragged through the cat-flap
in the door.
The steak went in the bin, and I took Caesar in.
How could I not?

Madalyn Morgan

OUR CATS

When we were young, my sister wanted to be a vet.
So she persuaded our parents to get a cat.
And another cat
And then our cats gave birth to more cats.
We gave some of them away.

One Christmas, when aunt Mary and uncle Harold visited,
I spent the nights sleeping on the sofa in the lounge
with five kittens skittering around the floor.

Later I started having attacks of asthma.
Eventually we realised it was the cats.
We excluded them from the main part of the house
and had them neutered.

Once I found Doke (mother cat) and Pascal (daughter cat)
in the garden playing a game:
Pascal quietly sneaked up on Doke
and then suddenly ran forward.
At the crucial moment, Doke jumped a foot in the air,
while Pascal ran underneath her and out the other side.
Then both cats turned round and the game continued.
I suppose it's all part of learning to be a cat.

The cats are all dead now.
Belle, the matriarch, died curled up in her cardboard
box
that my father had cut a gash in
so that the heating pipe went through the box.
He called it her centrally heated box.

As I remember, Pascal was hit by a car
in Lower Hillmorton Road.
One sunny day, Doke lay down in the warm sunshine
on the patio, and never got up.
She died as she lived: flopsy.

(*I know received opinion now is that domestic cats
should be neutered before they can reproduce.*)

Jim Hicks

MY CINQUAIN

A Cinquain has five lines - the first line of two syllables, increasing the number by two until the last line, which repeats the first line's number of syllables.

My cat:
My off-hand friend,
A peerless predator,
Quick co-ordinated killer:
Of mice.

Chris Rowe

MY CAT

My cat prowls everywhere
Across my table, under my chair
It may outwardly appear to be cuddly and cute
But lurking within is a cunning brute
It thinks I will welcome it into my house
If it offers me the carcass of a half-eaten mouse
It gently purrs and rubs round my ankles
It just wants feeding, that's what really rankles
I can seldom sit down and relax because
It leaps onto my lap and digs in its claws
It creeps round the garden intimidating birds
I won't mention what it leaves amongst my herbs
It sneaks in from the rain and proceeds to doze
On top of my clean, neatly ironed clothes
It scratches at my carpet and rips the curtains
It is determined and deceitful, that's for certain
If you are wanting a pet, a cat will not do
You can't own a cat, the cat will own you

Steve Redshaw

A CAT

A Matter of a Task to Ask the Fatness of a Cat

That cat, that on the mat sat,
Is he thin or is he fat?
He is such a fuzzy pussy
It's hard to tell anything like that.
You have to hurt his feline feelings,
Make a beeline for his tum,
his tail would be a fail.
But when he's in the rain,
though he thinks it's such a pain,
My task? Success with a soggy moggie!
So gladly, here ends my tale.

Philip Gregge

CAT

1

I sure was sold a pup when I got me
A bargain from the Cats' Home, almost free,
A pretty, stray cat, grateful for a home
Who'd snooze upon my bed and only roam
Around the neighbours' gardens to dispose
Quite sneakily - yet not disturb a rose -
The evidence that she had eaten well
On out-of-date meat Asda couldn't sell.
But no. Expensive manufactured muck
For cats is all she'll eat or rather suck
The jelly, leaving mouldering, drawing flies,
Those tiny chunks of yuk, rejected prize.

The papers on my desk are smudged by paws,
The legs of which are shredded by her claws.
And when it rains, then just inside the door
I place absorbent matting on the floor
Against her entry flap, but still a sheet
Displays the sodden imprint of her feet.
She leaves behind upstairs – I just can't win –
Bed-coverings like exotic leopard skin.
But when it's fine, especially at night,
She thunders down the stairs. I wake in fright.
Against one thing she's absolutely set -
The trauma of the visit to the vet.
First find your cat, then catch it, is the test.
A skilful hunter, one of nature's best,
Well understands evasion as the prey.
In Sisyphean effort waste your day.
To 'own' a cat's an unrewarding slog
So make your life much easier – get a dog!

2

At work all day, I thought I'd find a cat
A substitute replacement for a dog,
A furry, purring friend upon a mat.
Instead I got a Sisyphean slog
Of damage limitation in the house.
First, mopping up the imprint of its paws
(A harder task than charring for a spouse),
Then covering up the carving by its claws.
Then being woken in the early hours
When, dreaming, I've forgotten daytime cares,
A wayward fiend with preternatural powers
Goes thundering in pit-boots down the stairs.
This sonnet reinforces previous verse:
A dog's a friend for life – a cat's a curse!

Chris Rowe

BEING A CAT

A piece of nonsense written about a cat.

Sometimes I wish I was a cat
Although the one thing
I have no desire to do
(Let me make it clear from the start)
Is to stick my head between my legs
And gaily lick my parts!

I wish I could climb the curtains,
Hang on and swing, with pleasure so sublime
But I am afraid that, that way lies disaster!
Because my bulk would bring the curtains down
Along with all the plaster.

I wish I could circumnavigate the room via the back of
the sofa
To tear arse around from table to shelf, jumping all
over the furniture.
I would be full of fun and glee
But I am afraid that if I tried that
It would end in A and E.

I wish I could sit on the window ledge
Wearing nothing except my hair
Bringing a smile to passers by, who dared to stop and
stare.
But this would be with danger fraught
The Police would come and take me away and I
would end up in court.

I wish I could have my food put out
In a dish for me
Every morning of every day
My water refreshed regularly
I would have nothing to do but play

To hang and swing, to lunge and jump
To snuggle and sleep and purr
To lay down on a comfy rug with my tummy facing the
ceiling
Wearing only a lovely coat of fur
Oh, what a fantastic feeling.
So, as I lay here on my sheepskin rug
Curtains closed and fire warm
With my nakedness on display.
I hope no one knocks on the door
'cos I am being a cat today!

Linda Slate

THE MOUSE

Twas the week before Christmas, and all through the house,
creatures were stirring, but especially the mouse.
He scurried down the hall, and through the large door,
dodging people and pets, before skidding on the floor.
Inside the kitchen, was the food he sought.
He had to be quick, lest he be caught.
Up on the table, sat his greatest desire,
it was a Christmas pudding, being lit like a fire.
He licked his lips, and readied himself,
before turning around and climbing the shelf.
Up he went, careful and slick,
and started to wait, still as a brick.
A woman was there, serving food and drinks,
she was in the mouse's way, so he had to think.
He ran back to the door, and with all of his might,
he pushed and he shoved, and he closed the door tight.
The woman turned around, confused by the sound,
and when she moved the mouse jumped up from the ground.
With the woman distracted, he took the food and ran,
his pudding heist going according to plan.
His quest was over, and back to his hole he went,
in bed he lay, his day well spent.

Sophie Walters

THE FERRARI

Taxidermy. What a strange name!
And how society is divided by the dead animal game!
The ones with little hair, we don't mind if they
decease,
But the ones with hair all over, we seem to want them
to increase.

And the thicker is their hair, the more some hate or
love 'em;
Like badgers, in their setts, and the cullers up above
'em.
That bring us out in rages - in one way or the other;
You'd think that some of us are acting like their
mother.

This is strange, because the tiny humans we love to
cuddle
Are the little hair-less ones; aren't our minds a
muddle?
So we are inconsistent, not really a surprise,
When we're a single issue fanatic with only one thing
'fore our eyes.

Take my brother, our Harry, he always carried the
foremost flag.
Fighting with the opposition, trying to tear down their
rotten rag.
Yet when wifey saw a nice fur coat, and it was all
she'd ever liked,
His resolve collapsed completely and out to buy he
biked.

This all 'appened in London, wivin the sahnd of Bow
And soon 'arry and his wife were seen aht at a show.
His friends stood there astonished to see the compromise,
They couldn't adam and eve what was there before their eyes.

Shorely not! Wot's wiv the fur, 'arry?

Philip Gregge

LOCKDOWN PUPPY

*On hearing of great numbers of expensive dogs being
sold at the start of lockdown and the dog charities' fear of
rise in numbers at the end of it.*

The Lockdown puppy's specially bred
With coat of curly fur it cannot shed.
So clean in habits and easily fed,

With wide appealing eyes

With non-annoying, softly uttered bark
Ready for walkies' parade in the park,
Curling up neatly to sleep after dark.

And manageable size,

A new-fashioned dog, an up-to-date breed
A swankable dog – it's cash on a lead.
Whoever owns one has learned to succeed.

A costly canine prize.

The lockdown puppy's specially bred
That when the virus slows, then stops its spread,
Turns up obliging paws and drops down dead.

Chris Rowe

Press Pause

POT POURRI

THESE THINGS ARE SENT TO TRY US

These things are sent to try us,
And try us they surely do.
It's lots of tiny little things, like stones inside your
shoe.
Taken on their own and spread through several
years,
they would barely even register, let alone bring us to
tears.
But then there are those days – I know you know the
ones,
Where all those tiny little things decide to come in
tons.
You stub your toe, and burn the toast, and forget to
put the bins out,
Your knee is aching, you lost your keys – your sanity's
in doubt.
It's barely even lunchtime and your blood is on low
simmer
And someone is going to get it in the neck before
you get to dinner.
Is it him over there, chewing like a camel?
Or her on the sofa surfing every channel?
It could be stranger number 1, walking slower than a
snail.
"Come ooon, what are you doing? move your legs, let
sanity prevail!!!"
It could be stranger number 2, tap tapping against
your chair.
Keep it up, I dare you – your feet won't long be a pair.
Maybe stranger's number 3 and 4 are blocking up an
aisle
Because there's blatantly nowhere else to chat – just
breathe and try to smile

These things are sent to try us,
And try us they surely do.
It's the universe's way of telling us,
Stay home, grab a book, and pour a large one...or
two!

Terri Brown

EXPECTATIONS

Thump. Thump. The post Ah!
The post I had waited for so long
and almost given up listening for the sound.
Excitement growing as I realised that
this was really the parcel I had prayed for.
All the hard work, the hours on my own,
the family events I had missed to meet the deadline.
Dare I open the package?
Was my excitement ill-placed?
I had been so proud and so pleased that
at last I could share my thoughts with my friends.
I bent down and gathered the parcel in my arms,
it was heavier than I remembered.
Should I leave it for a while or take the plunge?
Let's have another coffee first.
How very silly this sounds and yet so much of my energy
and time had filled those blank sheets of paper.
That's enough coffee,
let's see what the post really brought this morning.
It really has been a surprise, and all I could think of,
all the trepidation I had felt and now the success I felt,
that warm feeling that I had made it.
My efforts had paid off
and my memories had been enjoyed by a publisher,
I hadn't really thought this was possible.
Now to enjoy that warm feeling...

Pam Barton

THE END

Meet me as an equal, Death,
Meet me in my den,
Let me chose the how and where,
And you can choose the when.

Let me not go by the road,
Smeared along the tar,
Or clutching at my aching heart
in some cheap bazaar.

It would be nice to say goodbye,
With family at my bed, and
play the end for all its worth,
Until they think I'm dead.

Then listen to their tears and wails,
And see who doesn't cry,
Before I feebly raise my hand,
And open just one eye.

"I'm going now," I'd croak again,
"The dark is drawing in,
Take me great redeemer,
To leave this world of sin."

Then I'd do my Shakespeare face,
Wrist against the head
"I go now to a better place ...
Whoops, I think I'm dead."

I jest oh Death so hear me now,
My life has been a riot,
But at the end I want to go,
In dignity and quiet.

Holidays are fun with friends,
And family (if you dare),
But journeys of transition
are a solitary affair.

Meet me as an equal Death,
Softly in my home,
And let us move on peacefully,
And very much alone.

Geoff Hill

SHAKESPEAREAN VERSE

When they received the urgent call
They all assembled in the hall.
The eldest daughter passed the test:
'Oh father king, I love you best.'
Her younger sister, rather sore,
Declared 'I love you even more.'
The youngest said, with deeper voice,
'There's no need now to make a choice.
I've formed a plan to cut out strife:
I'll not be any French king's wife.
P'rhaps I'm just a simple cynic –
I got altered at the clinic.
All future arguments I'll spare –
Me, your legal, masculine heir.
To cut out this unseemly fuss,
I've changed into Cordelius.'

Chris Rowe

PERFECT

Perfection is such a curious word.
Why would you want perfection?
Where is the challenge in that?
The thing I like most about you
Is that you have your faults.
That's what makes you perfect.

Perfection is such a lazy word.
In an ideal world things wouldn't be ideal.
What I really like is interesting.
Quirky, funny and full of charm.
And in there lies numerous faults.
That's what makes you perfect.

Perfection is such a deceptive word.
What we really strive for is fresh.
You can't beat that feeling of passion,
And that comes from rawness and grit,
And that comes from all your faults.
That's what makes you perfect.

Lindsay Woodward

BLESS US ALL

Bless us oh great architect
And keep us night and day
In church and mosque and synagogue
And anywhere we pray

But faith eludes so many more
No matter how we try
Confused and contradicted
On where the truth may lie.

Jehovah Jesus Allah Buddha
Revered by all so wise
Alas, I've found no golden road
That leads to paradise.

For I was cursed with a logical mind
Where two and two makes four
And laws of physics rule supreme
And yet I yearn for more

To me the 10 commandments
Cannot amount to naught
Though I prefer the 11th
"Thou shalt not get caught"

Jesus gave the beatitudes
At his sermon on the mount
Blessed are these and blessed are those
There were eight at my last count

But may I add another one
Before this poem's retired
"Blessed are those who just don't know
And even so are inspired."

Geoff Hill

MY SPOOKY HALLOWE'EN

It felt cold, like dead bones, something tickled my
face
It woke me. I froze. Just lay there. Staring into
darkness.
It happened again. I dare not move. What was it?
A spider's web,
I hadn't dusted it away, hanging, longer, longer
Then sharp finger nails bounced across my head,
tapping.
Frightening. Not a spider
I wanted to scream, dare not move, not a muscle.

Something scary was happening.
An unknown eeriness.
The night was dark, coal darkness.
No moon lighting the sky, no stars, nothing.
Think, where was I? Can't think, too scared
It happened again, in the deep darkness of night
Scratching my left cheek, sharp.

Eerily horrific. Not daring to move.
I wasn't in my bed, was I?
My hand slowly grasped my bed sheet,
It was quiet, too quiet. I dare not move another
muscle.
What was happening? Was it a nightmare?
A ghostly whirring sound echoed around my ears.

I froze. Not moving a muscle. Another scrape of a sharp nail.
A sharp metal nail or a skeletal nail on my cheek.
That's it. Too much. Must be my imagination running riot.
Halloween on the news, in the shops
I turned onto my side and cautiously reached for the side light.
Nothing there. It should be.
A switch placed at the side of a small set of bedside drawers.
I can't feel anything. Leaning further out of bed.
There it was again, a scratch on my hand.
Frightening.

No sound. Silence. I screamed, a long, slow, blood curdling scream.
A click. Light suddenly flooded the room.
Husband said: "Whatever is the matter? I told you not to eat cheese that late at night."

Kate A.Harris

THE DEFATIGABLE TOURIST

*This poem is a Villanelle: a poem of three-lined verses
where the first and third lines of the first verse are
repeated, changing positions to become the last line of
the next verse, and so on, until the last verse of four lines
where they come together in a conclusion of the theme
and rhyme scheme.*

There are some sights that should be missed:
At Presidential heads I groan.
I've shed them from my bucket list.

Where Juliet was never kissed,
I shall request not to be shown:
There are some sights that should be missed.

Wine-tastings are by me dismissed,
And sea-sick trips that make me moan.
I've shed them from my bucket list.

With little mermaids make no tryst –
For me no bronze or posing stone.
There are some sights that should be missed.

In tourist groups I'll not enlist:
There's always one shouts at a phone.
I've shed them from my bucket list.

On cruising ships I'll play no whist,
I'd sooner be at home alone.
There are some sights that should be missed
I've shed them from my bucket list.

Chris Rowe

HOW OUR GIFTS WERE RECEIVED

Written on seeing a painting of the Magi, in the Flemish style, in a Museum in Madeira while listening to a Mandolin concert.

The sparkle in his laughing eyes
Reflecting the glitter
Made mine the easiest gift to offer.
His small fingers examined the coins
Briefly.
When I had packed, dreaming of kings,
I had imagined crowns, orbs, rings.
In this bare house, I saw instead
My gold would buy essentials -
Wine and bread.

The room was suffused with perfume
When the seal of the second gift was broken.
All three breathed the fragrance
Of the frankincense.
Delightedly, the child clapped his hands.
A palpable presence of prayer
Wrapped them in mystery.

A strange change came over us
As the third present was proffered
Diffidently
Eagerly the child grasped this present.
Joseph and Mary gasped, caught their breath,
Knowing the contents represented death.
None of us could withstand
The child's troubled eye
As with a sigh
He fingered the myrrh.   **Sylvia Mandeville**

SONG FOR YOURSELF

I can stand up.
I can breathe in hard
and when the world curses me,
I'm laughing.
I can feel the hurricane
I can run to the ice cream van
and when the something under the bed howls at me,
I'm singing
I can fall like a feather,
I can punch like a jackhammer,
and when confused grey burdens me ...,
I'm dancing.
My ear can
accept any noise
My eye can
see across counties
My hands can
touch rainbows,
My nose can
sense goodness and,
My tongue
tell of it all.
I can hold love gently,
I can keep me to myself,
and when death is just a note on a wind chime,
I'm really living.

Chris Wright

A POEM FOR LOCKDOWN

Changes in Lockdown experiences to be sure!
Wash hands, 20 seconds, always, and more,
Keep your distance, two metres, minimum,
Antibacterial wipes until there's a cure.

Keep exercising, walk everyday if possible.
Eat healthily, no more thanks,
This virus will be beaten,
Note every move is traceable.

It will be worth all the restrictions,
Masks worn even when shopping.
Over 70s it will soon be your turn,
Protection from the virus with injections.

Hugging family or friends is not allowed, yet.
Think positive, happier times ahead,
Do not fret there's a future, Covid free,
Freedom to escape on that holiday jet.

Kate A.Harris

THE RING PULL

There are many things sent to try us,
especially in lockdown,
but the thing sent to try me the most
is the ring pull!
Rusty, they cut your finger
and leave you wondering
if your finger will turn septic or worse.
You break your nails lifting the ring
from the top of the tin to pull it.
It snaps off as you begin to pull it,
or, as one did the other night,
snap off when my tin of beans
was only a quarter open.
I tried using a regular tin opener,
but the lid was bent,
the wheel on the tin opener
was unable to get a grip
on the distorted lid,
so it kept going round and round
without making an impression.
The opening was too narrow to get a spoon in,
so I ended up hooking the baked beans
out with a wide-bladed knife.
During the sunny spell we had before Easter,
I fancied a cool drink of lemonade.
I took a can from the fridge, pulled on the ring pull,
and the top of the can flew off
spraying lemonade everywhere.
After cleaning up the kitchen – and a sticky me –
I poured myself a glass of wine.
There are no ring pulls on a bottle of McGuigan.

My worst experience with a dodgy ring-pull
was last night.
I decided to have a jacket potato
with tuna and sweetcorn.
The ring-pull on the sweetcorn
didn't quite remove the lid.
Draining the water off
I lost half the sweetcorn down the sink
because the lid was bent
and the sweetcorn escaped from the sides.
The ring-pull on the tuna stuck halfway,
so I gave it a good tug and the lid flew off,
covering my face and hair
with fish and sunflower oil.
In the end, I made a cheese sandwich.
No ring pulls on a cheese sandwich.

Madalyn Morgan

IT'S MY PANIC

Go and open the door
          No, I've lost my courage
          I'm terrified
          I'm in a panic.

Go and open the door
          Face my fears
          Don't be a wuzz
          I'm in a panic

Go and open the door
          I've fallen in the garden
          I broke my wrist. Help.
          I'm in a panic

Go and open the door
          My head's spinning
          I'm in a whizz
          I'm in a panic.

Go and open the door
          I want to stay indoors
          I need to be safe inside
          I'm in a panic.

Go and open the door
          I can't face the world head on
          Or change things I can't face
          It's my panic.

Go and open the door
   I've changed my dentist
   I've changed my optician
   I'm not in a panic.

Go and open the door
   I've moved house, all change
   I must find my courage
   I'm not in a panic, not now.

My door is now open
   I've faced new challenges
   I'm going on holiday, Dartmouth
   I'm not in a panic, not any more.

Kate A.Harris

FEEL THE FEAR

I wrote this poem after my first public performance of my Poetry. Feel the Fear and Do It Anyway is a book by Susan Jeffers.

Oh why, oh why did I agree to this?
I am terrified and I feel sick!

If you find yourself thinking these words
And you are not feeling very nice
May I make so bold as to offer you
This poetic piece of advice...

When everything seems to be going wrong
And your brain goes on strike and says 'so long'
When your nerve endings are buzzing everywhere
From the soles of your feet to the roots of your hair.

When your mouth is so dry
That your tongue swells and sticks,
When you really want to cry.
Your lips tingle, your cheeks burn and your eyes
sting!
When you think that you are going to die.

When you are paralysed
And you are rooted to the spot.
When you feel you just can't move,
Then your stomach joins in, with a gurgle and a pop!
And you wish you had eaten some food.

When your heart thunders inside your chest
At double, then treble then quadruple the speed.
When your eyes blur over, so you can't read the text
And you wish you could clear them with a blink.
Then your bladder joins the mayhem with an urgent need
And you wish you hadn't had that last drink.

When your muscles start jumping
And you are sure everyone can see.
When this place where you are
Is the last place you want to be.
When you silently wait for that hole to appear
To suck you up and take you away.
This is the moment when you are FEELING THE FEAR
But you are DOING IT ANYWAY

THEN...

When the shaking subsides
And your heartbeat calms
When your muscles relax
In your legs and your arms
When a small sip of water
Wets your mouth and frees your tongue
When you realise it's all over.
And it wasn't so long!
When your nerve endings chill and the hairs lay down
When in that moment you know that you SURVIVED
Know this...

Three minutes of TERROR every now and then
Reminds you that you are ALIVE

Now you are ready to do it again

To go through it all on another day
Now you understand what it means
TO FEEL THE FEAR AND DO IT ANYWAY

Linda Slate

SOUND SPINNER

A sonnet

Whirl me some words, witty spinner,
Knitting fine yarns so lustrously.
Weave me a tale of a winner.
Use ears as eyes; then make me see.
Lure me with fantasy phrases,
Enchanting word-weaver of sound.
Merge me in magical mazes,
Entice me to enter your ground,
Lead me on boldly in brave dance.
Stomp with strong foot verbal flora,
Seduce my ears with assonance.
Trip me with a slow caesura,
Picture-in-the-mind creator,
Wordsmith-worker, poem-maker.

Chris Rowe

VISITOR

Piles and piles of dirty washing,
Giant trainers in the corridor,
Empty beer bottles, empty cereal packets,
Crumpled towels in the bathroom,
Dumb-bells on the landing,
The miraculous simultaneous act of
sitting on the toilet and cleaning one's teeth,
The whispered telephone conversations,
Scooby-snacks after midnight,
The occasional spiky mood,
The football matches on the telly,
The lifts - here, there and everywhere.

These things are sent to try us parents -
For he is home from university.
These glorious things,
These wonderful things,
This marvellous mess,
This celebration of life bursting forth.

No, it will not last.
But let us wallow in its confusion,
For now.
For now.

John Howes

FERRARI

I'm a Ferrari. I vroom, therefore I am.
I like to think I'm a better representative
of the race of cars (no pun intended) than some,
but I spend much of my time in the garage
in the dark, contemplating my existence.
Still, I shouldn't complain:
some work cars have a much harder life than mine,
and how some company cars are treated
doesn't bear thinking about.
In times past,
we had a difficult relationship with humans,
what with being driven into other cars and buildings,
but we're a bit safer now.
Or so they say.
Now, humans complain that we're smelly
and pollute the air.
Some humans don't like us much at all.
Well, the feeling's mutual.
Many humans seem to think
the whole car is a rubbish bin.
And I don't even want to consider
what my previous owners were doing
on my back seat.
Something to do with their baby, I think.
So, much of the time I can use
to ponder my own life cycle.
We Ferraris are often better maintained
than family cars, so I can't complain.
I always feel better after an oil change.
I'll have a longer working life than most. And
eventually I shall dwindle and go to the scrapyard.

Jim Hicks

BALLOONS

A transient thing is a balloon
A provider of fun and decoration
For just one day

What happens to the balloons
That go home with party attendees
Are they treasured

What happens to the balloons
That break free from small inept fingers
And float away

A wonderful thing is a balloon
A thin rubber casing filled with breath
Or helium

Is there a world where lost balloons
Live free and find their sanctuary
Until their end

Is there a world where lost balloons
Can throw off the yoke of the trailing string
And the weight

A beautiful thing is a balloon
A short-lived giver of joy and fun
For just one day

EE Blythe

I'M A NOTICE SHEET FAILURE

Look! Everyone but me has a Notice Sheet!
I'm really not sure when I started noticing the Notices
on the Notice Sheet were escaping my notice.
They say to me, "It was a Notice on the Notices",
but the noticeability of the Notices on the Notices
seems to have grown noticeably less noticeable of
late.

In fact so unnoticeable that you'll have noticed
I noted I didn't even notice when I stopped noticing
the Notices.
And now I notice that I'm suffering the consequences
of the lack of noticeability of the Notices.
There are things I notice happening
which I notice I should have noticed earlier,
but now I notice only when it's too late.

If only the Notices were easier to notice!
Then I could make some notes about the noteworthy
notices.
Maybe whoever gives us the Notices should give us
more notice
they are going to give us the Notices,
because often, the Notice-giver doesn't even notify
us
they are going to give us the Notices.

The Notices are sprung on us entirely without
notification
and I don't even notice because I'm still noticing
what I was noticing before the Notices,
and what I need to notice after the Notices.
So the Notices on the Notice Sheet whizz by...
...unnoticed.

Philip Gregge

QUAD POEM

This poem consists of four verses of four lines, each with four words of four letters.

Take path, pass farm:
Moor, peak, tarn - calm.
Duck, coot, huge swan.
Then mist. View gone.

Dull, feel lost. Rain!
Tire, fall, ouch! Pain.
Want help, must cope,
Slow plod with hope.

Trip, oops, stub toes.
Cave, rest, alas! Doze...
Wake cold. Dark. Fear.
Luck! Moon. Path near.

Whew! Ache. Trek down.
Soon back into town.
Home. Bath, glow rosy,
Soup, warm, safe, cosy.

Chris Rowe

EACH AND EVERY DAY

What makes the day better?
What makes the day survivable?
Well, each and every day, you could...

READ a page of P.G. Wodehouse
LISTEN to a song sung by Frank Sinatra
LEARN a new word in French and put it into a
sentence
DRINK, slowly, a cup of carefully-made coffee
WRITE another sentence or paragraph of your latest
poem or memoir
SPEND five minutes meditating on a sentence of
ancient scripture
PAY a compliment to someone either in person or on
social media
DISCOVER the story of someone in the world who is
suffering and work out some small way to help them
WATER a flower or just admire one
SING a song from a musical that makes you feel
different
SHARE a picture of somewhere wonderful you have
been and be thankful for that experience
PLAN a new trip in detail, even if you never get there
DWELL on the good moments in relationships and
forget the bad
DECIPHER a complicated piece of jazz by listening to
it twice, maybe three times
SEND a message to someone you haven't heard from
for a while, even if they never send one to you
THINK only the best of people, if you can
BUY a Big Issue because it makes a huge difference
to that person
SMILE at someone in the street, even when you don't

feel like it
TREAT your body by giving it something really
healthy to eat
SAY something friendly to a person in a shop who
serves you, it might make them feel better

You may not do all of these things.
But even one of these things
Could make your day better.

John Howes

WHEN THE DARK EYES COME

Can you tell
I'm scared as hell
Of what may come today

Dark or light
Nothing is right
Life is a game you play

Round and round
Treading old ground
Keep the real world at bay

Hang your head
Don't cut me dead
To not hear what I say

Can't you see
I'll never be
The one to fly away

But you did
From me you hid
For you chose not to stay

EE Blythe

OUT FROM UNDER THE CARPET

I wrote this to try to describe what depression and post-traumatic stress disorder feels like.

The Darkness falls upon me
Like a heavy dusty old carpet.
I am knocked to the floor.
I gasp for breath
Suffocating under the heaviness and the darkness.

I lay down in submission
I lay down in the stifling dark.

I close my eyes to have my own darkness.

I open my eyes and I choke
It's too heavy
Too dark
I am too small
I am too weak to fight it off.

I close my eyes to have my own darkness.

I open my eyes and I choke
The weight is so heavy on my back
I can't breathe, I can't get up.

I close my eyes to have my own darkness.

I open my eyes and I choke
I know I must get out
Out from under this heaviness
Out from under this darkness.
I begin to drag myself in search of some light.

I know the light is beyond the edge of the carpet.

It is taking such a long time
It is such hard work.

I must keep my eyes open
I must keep on fighting

I must get out from under the carpet

Linda Slate

CHEER UP!

Sometimes I wake up and there is nothing there,
my mind is full of empty,
I'm bearing a heavy load of dark,
like I've been pushed down into the ground
and told to stay there,
not speaking,
not thinking,
not hoping,
not being.

Ladies and gentlemen, this is depression.
I didn't choose it, despite what you think.
I have so much to live for,
So many reasons to be cheerful,
But I am like this today
And all I can do is wait to be freed.
You must know, it's not deliberate,
It's nothing personal,
I hate this black dog as much as you.
But I can't just snap out of it.

And the worst thing you can say,
The very worst thing you can say is
"Cheer Up",
As if I hadn't thought of that already.

John Howes

SERIOUS STUFF

Humour is a serious business
Whether you giggle or guffaw
It's the toughest writing genre
But not one to ignore

I'm rubbish at telling jokes
But have a few stock gags
They are pretty puerile
But I'll send up warning flags

I do enjoy a Limerick
Of that there is no doubt
It's serious , comedy writing
Poetry rules, don't flout!

Not sure about stand up
Stick to a script, no thanks
I'd probably spoil the gags
And tumble to the ranks

So, I'm happy writing doggerel
You know, this kind of stuff
I can write as quick as you like John,
Hope that's enough!

Paul Clark

ANDERSON COUNTRY

Terranians! The millennium nears
But teatime TV for 30 years
Showed Supermarionation fun
From Anderson's Century 21.
Wonderful sounds for a children's show
Like Stingray's drums or Thunderbirds are go!
"Battle Stations!" calls the Tower,
"Anything can happen in the next half hour!"
Martians made their first attack,
Relaying instructions was Captain Black.
Marina was my pin-up choice
With the perfect female speaking voice.
Fireball glowed with re-entry heat
Now XL5's just a spreadsheet.
With UFOs they couldn't ignore
And Straeker's office is on which floor?
Four Feather Falls where cowboys creek
Or a nine year old saves the world each week.
The Moon pulls away and roams the sky
Or a model model-T goes speeding by
And a jet is launched from a submarine
Where a fish is judge of a human being
Or palm trees swoon for a jumbo jet;
Men fall twenty storeys and don't break a sweat;
Rockets can race to the heart of the Sun,
And a woman's place is a MIG21.
Gerry and Sylvia's VistaVision lands
Where the only thing real is the shot of the hands.
X-Files follows its weekly fad
two puppets chasing someone's dad
No resolution; just one of those things
We never find out who's pulling the strings.

Just use your Brains and find Harmony
The truth is out there and it's FAB.

Chris Wright

Note from Chris: Radio 4's programme was about the other Gerry Anderson. I hope this does not spoil your enjoyment of the above too much.

A KYRIELLE

A Kyrielle is a French verse form in short usually octosyllabic rhyming couplets often paired in quatrains and characterised by a refrain which is sometimes a single word or sometimes the full second line of the couplet or fourth line of the quatrain.

Oh what the hell's a kyrielle?
It's something I can't even spell,
More puzzle than a poem
I'll just try to show'em
And hope my effort goes down well

Oh no you fool, I am so thick
I've done it wrong, it makes me sick
I am a dolt
My scheme's at fault
It's nothing but a limerick.

So here goes then – a second time
At making use of words that rhyme
– But my rhythm isn't right
I'm in quite a sticky plight
And plainly quite well past my prime.

But now at least the end's in sight
And now at last I've got it right.
Run up the flag and ring a bell
For now I've made a kyrielle!

For I've worked hard throughout the night
And slogged away without respite
I knuckled down for quite a spell
And I have made a kyrielle.

For inspiration solved my plight
And I am reading with delight
For into place the words all fell
So that I made a kyrielle.

I did not find the effort slight
Although my mood was often light
For my self-doubt I learned to quell
And so I made a kyrielle.

So reaching out to all I tell
With repetition like a knell
That I've just made a kyrielle,
For struggling makes some things go well
So listen to my kyrielle.

Chris Rowe

SHREDDED KEATS

Who hasn't tried to learn a poem
but not many are still
trying and failing after 45 years!

"Why do we have to learn this, Mr Mills?"
then to be examined in the gymnasium
with the fifth formers sitting their O-levels
Now I look back and see this as the start of affection
for poetry
KEATS
Ode to Autumn
English teachers come and go
Mr Mills came and went too
PG Wodehouse with a nose like a beef tomato

"Wright why are you shouting?
I'll tell you why.
Con-dit-ion-ed reflex!"

it's Fruit of Activity with Songs
 three stanzas taking me a lifetime to learn

the first is a cornucopia of beautiful images and fruit
and finally, the wonderful bees you dream about and
never forget

the second you fall for a beautiful woman
part Kate Bush part Egyptian queen part harvest
goddess

stanza 3 is cacophony: Swallows and lambs and
Robins and crickets and gnats
These last noisy vectors I stole for one of my hymns
to the encroaching seas

Why can't I learn that last verse?
is it that I'm not interested?
My teacher didn't ask nicely
Learnt, the words become you

You love me love her love

The great mother

Are we so estranged from John Keats' world of
nature that
we can't see the woods or the trees
we can't see the cottages surrounded by ripe apple
orchards
and bees grown fat on the last rose blooms
or can't hear the redbreast nor the treble soft
every year I give myself the whole of autumn to learn
that final verse which softens the hibernal blow
Of cold, early, scarified winter
every year a few lines closer wish me luck
my dear writer friends
my plus, my minus and my equals

Chris Wright

Press Pause

PAST

CHARITY WALKING

For a breast cancer charity.

Walking, walking, walking.
5 Kilometres to go.
Feet rolling, feet rolling
Heel to toe, heel to toe.
Arms swinging
Mind singing
Blood pumping in my ears.
Dust stinging my eyes
Little dusty tears.

Walking, walking, walking.
4 Kilometres to go
Deep breathing, keep breathing
Find the rhythm, not too slow.
Mind racing
Thoughts pacing
Thoughts about the ones
Who have gone before
The ones we are all walking for.

Walking, walking, walking
3 Kilometres to go
Memories growing, memories flowing of the ones
I will see no more.
Of Debbie so beautiful
Of Debbie so strong
Dear Debbie I haven't seen you
For so very long.

Walking, walking, walking
2 Kilometres to go
Memories growing, memories flowing
Of a flame that burned so bright
Of Tina a fighter
Of Tina a true and gentle friend
Dear Tina
Dear Tina
Always cheerful to the end.

Walking, walking, walking
1 Kilometre to go
Memories coming, memories going
Of 2 boys without a Mother
Of Samina, Zuber's wife
Of Samina, the love of her husband's life
Dear sweet Samina
Too young
Far too young.

Walking, walking, walking
At the end now
Slowing down
Breathing slow, breathing low
Warm and satisfied in the after glow
For you my friends
For your families
For the loved ones you left behind
I walk every year for you
I walk and remember

Linda Slate

I CAN'T REMEMBER WHAT IT WAS

Why did I walk into the sitting room?
I don't think it was to write or zoom.
Not the phone, it wasn't ringing
I wasn't going to be singing.
Think laterally, that's what I've heard
Don't think of anything too absurd
What time of day is it? Look for clues.
The telly isn't on, so it isn't the news.

Why did I walk into the sitting room?
I've a cup of tea, without a spoon.
As I don't take sugar, I look elsewhere
There's one shoe, is it the spare?
The duster's on the table, is it needed?
Is the table dusty, or is the garden weeded?
Think again logically, I'm inside
In whom may I confide?

Why did I walk into the sitting room?
It's rather embarrassing in the dark and gloom.
I turn around looking for clues.
Ah, what's on the tele, it is the news.
I sit down on the settee, feeling comfortable
And not as before, when I felt vulnerable
In came the husband to check up on me
I'm sitting there as relaxed as could be.

I really can't remember what it was
So I sat down and gulped down the Shiraz
What happened to that, I couldn't think.
Must now put my glass in the sink.
Now I remember the thing that is the link
My husband smiles with a jaunty wink
It's tea that needs to be cooked
Everything is laid out ready. I just looked.

Kate A. Harris

DEMENTIA LAND

Welcome to dementia land
It's where I'm camped right now
On the outskirts of this town
I'm a visitor, for now

Memory seems to have flown away
It can't be found at all
Where are my spectacles
Have I left them in the hall?

They weren't in the hall
So I had a little think
Up the stairs again
They're in the kitchen sink

Have I got bread in the bread bin
Better look and see
Nothing in here but tomatoes
Oh lovely and a slice of Brie

I wondered where I left it
It was due to go in a wrap
All this activity
So now I need a nap!

Paul Clark

LEAP YEAR - TO BE SURE

Following an old Irish legend of a conversation between
St Bridget and St Patrick. Lent approaches, during which
no-one may marry. If a maid is unwed when Lent starts, it
will become obvious that she hasn't been asked.

Spoke Bridget to Patrick, "The women have said,
'You men are too slow to ask us to wed.

You profess your love, for a kiss - or two,
Then silence reigns. We know not what to do!'"

Said she, "Lent approaches; the whole town will know
That these maids are unwed; they have no ring to
show.

So hear, Father Patrick, they seek a tradition
To ask a man to his face to relieve their condition."

Said Patrick, "A hard thing you ask men to do,
But - a day every seven years? Would that satisfy
you?"

"Seven years?" cried the maid, "And only one day?
'Tis far too little; perhaps we should pray!"

And pray they did, right fervently.
They spoke with their Lord, and they rose from their
knee,

Then said Saint Bridget, "Now hear what I say!
It will be every four years - and not only one day!

The Lord has told me, on the whole leap year,
We may ask as we please and we'll shed not a tear.

So will you obey me, Patrick, called Saint?"
Patrick turned pale and his voice grew faint.

"Of course, good wench, when you put it that way.
If you say, 'God has told me!' who am I to gainsay?"

Philip Gregge

THE GHOST

Last night as I took my stroll
Along the canal side path
A figure came towards me
Pointing at the quay

He got closer and made a bow
Doffed his cap and smiled
Pointing at a lockgate
A faded copper plate

His features became sad
His shoulders drooped
Without a sound he turned around
Nodded and walked away

Paul Clark

FUN-SIZE

A4 was a polypocket
Before it was a children's locket
C change a word to keep afloat
D light's a poet's rowing boat

Chris Wright

FORGOTTEN

Forgotten fruit
Left hanging on the vine
Too old, and soft
Wrinkled
Withered with the cold
Shrunken by time
Ignored
No longer of use
Not overlooked, deliberately left
Rejected
Rattling with the dried leaves
Autumn glow to Winter frost
Forgotten

EE Blythe

I CAN'T REMEMBER

I know I should have done it,
But I can't remember what it was.
It was in my head when I lay in bed,
But I can't remember what it was.
It was something quite important,
Or so it seemed right then.
But can I remember what it was?
O drat! I've forgotten again!

I know I should have bought it,
But I can't remember what it was.
It was right at the top when I went in the shop,
But I can't remember what it was.
It was something I really needed,
I'm pretty sure of that,
But can I remember what it was?
I've forgotten again! Oh drat!

I know I should have sent it,
But I can't remember what it was.
That letter to Flo, or was it Joe?
I can't remember what it was.
They really needed an answer,
By yesterday, or before,
But can I remember what it was?
I've forgotten again! What a bore!

I know I should have fixed it,
But I can't remember what it was.
That thing, it's the same as that other wossname.
No, I can't remember what it was.
I'm sure something awful will happen
It it doesn't get fixed fairly soon.
But can I remember what it was?
I've forgotten again! What a goon!

I'll have to go back to where I knew for sure:
Upstairs, the other room, through that door.
Recreate the conditions for the fog to lift.
Perhaps another drink would make it shift?
Oh yes! I'll have another tot!
Then I can give it a further shot...
That's better! I'm sure to remember soon.
Maybe I'll have it this afternoon?...

No that didn't help, it's not coming back,
Maybe this is a permanent lack
Of remembering things that I shouldn't forget,
I didn't think I would lose it yet,
But there it goes, my memory;
I took it for granted, now I see...

But wait! It was shopping I needed to do!
And, oh yes! It was yeast I needed too!
And it was Joe, not Flo, I needed to mail,
To help with how to brew his ale.
And I should have fixed that beer-pulling tap,
The one which has had a slight mishap.

Look at that! My memory is quite intact.
I think I remember every fact!
Of all that's happened I'm totally sure,
And things which haven't, I remember those more!
And brewing and drinking, I know all about,
I'm glad old Joe will try it out.
Then I'll go round his and take my fixed tap
To pull the ale of that excellent chap.

And as we sit there we'll gently fade
Into somnolence with his ale's good aid.
Then - when we awake and try to recall
We'll find we can't remember at all:
Who we are, where we've been,
What we've done, what we've seen...
We'll just sit there, content as can be,
What use will we have for memory?

Philip Gregge

THERE WAS A TIME

Do you remember that 60's summer sun?
The frog-eyed Sprite and setting out for Spain?
The tree-lined roads through Franco?
The steely heat of Carcasonne
And rough red wine beneath a shadowy tree?
The traffic cops in black who trailed us for a while?
The camping on a council's rubbish dump
And tent pegs you had freely left behind?
The locals roughed up the soil around their tents
To keep out "vipers" in the night

Once into Spain the road was rough
We hoped the Guardia Civil would help us on our way
But this was Franco's Spain and we were wrong.
At last the huddled white of Estartit
A bit less glorious than we'd planned
Its two streets powdered red with dust
The season's Costa Brava tune thumped out
From waking to the end of night.
Bikini busting girls slid by
Though most were far too young for us
Or we too old for them
But we found Anne and one we called "the Queen"
Both older, posh, experienced and fun.
And these were sweet times nonetheless
With unexpected joys and scents
Spiced plates and lazy wine.
It had no permanence I know
It was of candy-floss and card
But sometimes when I wake up in the night
I am still there.

Keith Marshall

TELEVISION IN THE SEVENTIES

Farewell
to all those memories,
of 70s TV shows,
Farewell
to Morecambe and Wise,
to Derek Hobson's ties,
Farewell
to Top of the Pops,
to King of the Cops,
Farewell
to Sunday teatime Dickens,
and Tom Good's hand-reared chickens,
Farewell.

Those were the days we will treasure in our hearts,
Those were the times I will always think of you.

Farewell
to Starsky and Hutch,
to Jerry, Tom and Butch,
Farewell
to Ironside's wheelchair,
to Leo Sayer's hair,
Farewell
to Harbin's origami,
to Mainwaring's Dad's Army,
Farewell
to Kojak's famous lolly,
to Daisy Duke (oh golly!)
Farewell

Those were the days we will treasure in our hearts,
Those were the times I will always think of you.

Farewell
to Rising Damp and Rigsby,
to the biggest dog called Digby,
Farewell
to foons and sporks from Noakes,
to Peter Purves' jokes,
Farewell
to Frank Bough and Eddie Waring,
to Evil Knievel's daring,
Farewell
to Bunty James and How!
James Herriot and that cow,
Farewell

Those were the days we will treasure in our hearts,
Those were the times I will always think of you.

Dickie Davies, Frank Cannon,
Shari Lewis, Angela Rippon,
Kent Walton, Lesley Judd,
David Nixon, David Coleman,
Fred Dinenage, Ali Bongo,
Petrocelli, Susan Stranks...

I will remember you,
Good luck in all you do.
Farewell.

John Howes

I CAN'T REMEMBER

I'm standing at the checkout, laying out my goods,
Carrots and potatoes, a joint of meat, because
We are having friends to dinner, they're rather picky
about their food,
Something else I had to buy - but can't remember
what it was!

I'm waiting at the traffic lights and I am in a rush.
It seems to take for ever and I think I'm going to
swear.
Ah! the lights turn green, I gently rev, but I don't let
out the clutch.
I know I'm driving into town, but can't remember
where!

I meet a friend for coffee, haven't seen him for a
while.
We talk of family and work, and if we're happy with
our lot.
We chat away for hours and put the world to rights.
One thing I just had to tell him, but couldn't remember
what!

I'm climbing up the stairs, getting rather out of breath.
My knee-joints ache, my feet are sore, I think I feel a
stitch.
I need to pause and rest a while, I'll soon regain my
strength.
Now, was I going up or down? I really don't remember
which!

Steve Redshaw

SLIPPING, SLIPPING

The clock flew twice round the room
And slipped through a slightly open window
Time was gone
The time was gone
And so were you

Lifeless. Still and cold. Grey dawn
Slipping through planes of other places
Silent scream
The silence goes on
And so do you

Black clouds
Dark skies
Purpling mists
Cloud thinking

Building the jigsaw of now
Each piece slips into the right space
Space made whole
The spaces gone
And so for you

The clock sits back on the wall
A slip, still, of vibrating time
Drops in place
The drop is done
And this is you

White clouds
Blue skies
Long views
Clear thinking

The clock sits back on the wall
And the jigsaw is whole, once more

EE Blythe

REMNANTS

As once in open wild
He swings his old time haversack
With yellow braces flying
And climbs up to his roost
An old worn plastic chair

An open lounge for residents
Used cups without their saucers lie around
Grey tufts of cardigans, white tufts of hair
A man in purple trousers takes a seat

A frozen loop before the large TV
Where no one speaks
But hunchified lean out
While staff in blue make pirouettes
Around the silent chairs

So join the queue
You will not wait for long
These papery ghosts
Will quietly lead your hands

Keith Marshall

TREASURE UNBURIED

I've often wondered on Armistice day
Whether cubs and scouts had a role to play?
It seems they did in the heat of wars
Directing fire engines and delivering stores

This I found in Facebook just now
Scouts, guides and cubs , you take a bow!
You might be heroes, you might not
Thankfully no bombs or fires to plot

Hear these lost tales of mystery
Your roots so deep in history
Some things can never be repaired
I'm sure you'll always be prepared!

Paul Clark

MY COUNTRY TALE

I loved singing 'I wheeled my wheelbarrow
Through streets broad and narrow'.
Only four, singing along the village path
I loved climbing trees, that sprawling yew tree
The danger. I never fell. It was a possibility.

I loved catching squirmy tadpoles.
Taking my jar tied around
With string to swish in the brook.
Where were the tadpoles?
Just creepies caught and let go,
Sticklebacks, small fish, yes.

Father collected mushrooms in the field
The size of a dinner plate.
Where did he find them? Which field?
He would cook them, one at a time
Fried in butter, take out the mushroom
Fried bread, crispy, mushroomy, yum.
Where are the mushrooms now?

I loved walking up the quiet lane,
A favourite walk to Fox Hole Bridge.
The brook where I played Poohsticks.
With my two young sons, Tony and Chris.
Throwing lengths of sticks too big to float
Not too big to stick in muddy water.
From one side to the other side of the bridge,
In a fast flowing brook, with luck
My stick would be first to the other side.

Run back over the bridge, another stick
Poohsticks was repeated again, again and again.
Great fun, perhaps not as exciting for them?
As simple fun enjoyed in the 50s and 60s.
Continue walking slowly, observing,
Up the lane, summer overgrowth.

I loved the flowers, red campion
Buttercups, rosebay willow herbs, ferns.
I loved the colours, wildflowers everywhere.
Overgrown hedges each side of the lane,
Rustlings in the hedge, what's there?

A blackbird scratching for grubs,
Maybe a hedgehog, nothing to see.
I loved the small spinney, primroses.
Dark, mysterious, fairy imaginings,
Only in books, not real, were they?

Walking further around the sharp corner,
What's there, what's around the corner?
I loved the steep hill, climbing,
Climbing, a crop of wheat on one side,
Swaying in the breeze, this way, and that.
Horses grazing in the paddock on the other side.

Climbing to the top, nearly there
Top of the hill, tired legs, turn around
I loved the panoramic view.
Fields, distant fields, a faraway town,
Houses, ripe arable corn, cattle grazing.

A small village in the Welland valley,
The church, our house, views.
I'd always loved walking, so did father
Perhaps I should return to walk that walk.

Kate A.Harris

HADDOCK

Poached smoked haddock for tea
With bread and butter cut fancy
Rice pudding waiting in the oven
It's a hospital day meal
My hospital day
Twice a week for physiotherapy
All so that when I grow up
My head will be upright

EE Blythe

LOCKDOWN PASTA

Zoom, pasta, clearing out the freezer
And why we wanted all those loo rolls.

The corners up above go whirling round
As gingerly I sit and smile for Zoom
And now my head is spinning with the room.
That packet in the freezer that I found,
Squashed up and out-of-date and at the back:
Anchovies - eaten with infrequency
Bestow an unexpected piquancy -
The one ingredient that I feared to lack.
They make a tasty paste for boring pasta.
So proud I was when I served up that dish,
Tomatoes, basil - and a hint of fish.
But I'd created culin'ry disaster.
Lockdown-enforcing domesticity
Can cause at times some infelicity.

Chris Rowe

ANNIVERSARY XX

Remember when when she gave us the poem
Great writing, talking about our wedding
how everyone came the cakes were
Swimming, disco of indigo
you smiled all day
to you it seems a long time ago;
to me like last Tuesday

20 years! You get less than that for embezzlement
Our love book is reconciled and wonderful
your love emolument
my repayment is pitiful

So remember lisianthus
the exquisite bridal flowers
life's meaning handed to us
love isn't caged by the hours

Chris Wright

THE SUBSTANCE OF MEMORIES

Memories are often your most precious possessions.

I have a clock on my mantle,
That is right only twice a day.
I have a too small dress in my wardrobe,
I just can't bear to throw away.
I have a book on my bookcase,
I have read a hundred times.
Every time I read it,
There is so much more between the lines.
I have an old tin on my shelf,
Dark green, and battered
Filled with buttons and things.
I have a secret place in my bedroom,
Where I keep my Mother's and Grandmother's rings.
I've got knicknacks and doodads and wotnots,
Kept in a box under my bed.
These are all the substance of memories,
That keep the past alive in my head.

Linda Slate

THE NIGHT VISITOR

'Twas on the stroke of midnight,
the wind howled all around,
the ivy on the window tapped
and snow lay on the ground.

Far down the hill, the little town
had closed up for the night.
No music from the harbour inns,
no voices heard, no light.

Up on the cliff, above the waves,
the abbey stood on high,
its jagged walls a skeleton
against the moonlit sky.

And in the churchyard lay the bones
of sailors lost at sea,
washed up on the beach below
or fished out by the quay.

Some said upon the midnight hour,
church bells rang out clear,
then spirits rose up from their graves
and lovers fled in fear.

Some said 'twas haunted by a dog.
Some said they'd heard it howl.
On moonlit nights among the stones
some swore they'd seen it prowl.

Some stories said that vampires flew,
screeching round the hill,
but these were told by drunken sots.
Believe it if you will.

But, what happened here last night,
will surely you appal,
for I live in the manor house
against the churchyard wall.

The room was dark, the candle gone,
the fire was nearly dead.
I locked and bolted both the doors
and went upstairs to bed.

'Twas on the stroke of midnight,
the bells were ringing out,
the latch was rattled on my door.
I woke up with a shout.

The door creaked open, in it came,
a wailing broke the air,
enough to rend the hardest heart,
so heavy 'twas with care.

A figure stood upon the floor,
clothed all in ghostly white.
The wailing creature nearer came,
a truly fearful sight.

I'm cold, I'm cold, the spectre howled.
I'm cold, I'm cold, it said,
I'm cold, it moaned, *I'm freezing cold.*
I'm coming into bed.

The blankets lifted, in it slid.
It kicked, it turned, it tossed.
Its hands on me were blocks of ice,
its feet were like the frost.

It put its body close to mine.
Its bones were thin and frail.
The moonlight through the curtains shone
on features tired and pale.

The hours passed, the bells struck three,
I hadn't slept one jot.
I lifted up my sleeping son
and put him in his cot.

Wendy Goulstone

MINES AND MEMORIES

Both are just below the surface
Both are on the rise
The first we spot with eyes
Second never dies

Some mines are found
On a beach, in a wood
Or by a drone
Many more are sown

Cropping all year round
A most pernicious weed
It chokes out life
Dark memories are rife

November the 11th
From 1917
Memories and mines
Still a danger in modern time

Paul Clark

CHRISTMAS FAIRY

A pantoum is a Malaysian verse form which
comprises a series of quatrains, with the second and
fourth lines of each quatrain repeated as the first and
third lines of the next.

I stand at the top of my tree
Beneath are dark branches of green,
There's tinsel that turns in the air.
Twisting and twinkling, light dazzles.

Beneath are dark branches of green,
Glistening and glittering, globes glimmer.
Twisting and twinkling light dazzles.
Through dark the shining stars shimmer.

Glistening and glittering globes glimmer.
The cascades of light coruscate,
Through dark the shining stars shimmer.
In joyfulness I scintillate.

The cascades of light coruscate.
Serene, I gleam, I beam - that's me.
In joyfulness I scintillate.
I stand at the top of my tree.

Chris Rowe

A CHRISTMAS BLESSING

Months and years will come and go,
Old customs bow to new,
But forever is the love
My spirit holds for you.

And, whatever lies ahead,
Though I may be far away,
I will always love you
As I do, this Christmas Day.

Geoff Hill

A XMAS TRIFLE

This recipe makes a Xmas delight:
One juicy red apple tempting and bright
A handful of beans ambitious for height
Three bowlfuls of oats, a nourishing sight
A golden goose egg to help someone's plight
A shape-shifting pumpkin that speeds through the
night
Gingerbread housing an oven that's tight.
Mix all together to give it some bite.
And have you all guessed the clues in these rhymes?
The ingredients in our pantomimes.

Answers: Snow White, Jack and the Beanstalk, Goldilocks and the Three Bears, Mother Goose, Cinderella, Hansel and Gretel.

Chris Rowe

THE POETS

Pam Barton began writing again recently after many years. She has, in the past, had a radio programme for children, been a D.J. and put through the landing on the moon for the Australian Radio in the Indian Ocean. On returning to England, she was a busy parent with John, and became a skin care consultant up to District Manager. After moving again, she went to Luton University for a marketing course. She retired to Rugby with John. Now she is enjoying writing again, painting is also a great pleasure although, as with the writing, hard work is needed.

EE Blythe is compelled to write. And that's all that needs to be said.

Terri Brown – voice actor, artist and author – does not have a book that got her into reading because she doesn't remember a time when she didn't read. Her mother boasts that Terri was reading the likes of Jane Eyre at age seven. First published in a local newspaper aged nine, she caught the writing bug... she just had some things she needed to do first. A few decades, many adventures and a life less ordinary later, financed largely by freelance writing, she has now published her debut fiction novel, Shadow Man, which is available from Amazon.

Paul Clark has recently moved to Rugby and has found the abundance of Roman roads, canals and other historical sites and landmarks great inspirations for his writing. His genres include: poetry, short stories and a few magical realism novels in progress. He still maintains his links with Fantastic Writers; a group of creative writers with whom he has collaborated with on a number of anthologies entitled Fantastic writers and where to read them and Down the Inkwell.

He enjoys attending live mic poetry readings and the Hay festival is already in his diary next year. He hopes to attend as a writer one day!

Paul teaches functional skills, that's English and maths to apprentices. In a previous life, he has been involved in gardening in roles as a head gardener but his most interesting role was as the assistant head gardener at Luton Hoo golf and spa, a five star hotel which boasts landscape designed by Capability Brown.

Wendy Goulstone began writing plays from the age of four when given a model theatre, then for performing in story-time in primary school, where she was encouraged by a wonderful headmaster who introduced her to poetry. When eleven years old, she wrote a dramatised version of Little Women and a novel about a group of theatre-mad children. She directed plays at teacher training college, lived in Australia and New Zealand for four years, and on return to UK, studied for a BA with the Open University and became a member of Rugby Theatre and several writing groups. She continues to write short plays and organises Open Mics for poets and singers. Several of her poems have been published in literary magazines and anthologies and one won *The Oldie* poetry competition!

Philip Gregge was an optician in Rugby for over forty years. After qualifying as an optometrist, he studied theology. As part of the leadership team of a local charismatic church, he enjoys teaching Theology and has written a Theology training manual for study groups. He answers theological questions in 'Let's Ask Phil', letsaskphil.org

Philip started writing Historical Fiction after waking from an anaesthetic with a plot of an Anglo-Saxon murder mystery in his head. This whetted the fascination he already had for the early Dark Ages, and his research led him to write and publish 'Denua, Warrior Queen'; 'based on real history, but with some of history's intriguing blanks filled in'.

He is now working on a trilogy with his original murder mystery as the first part. In his spare time he plays the banjo in an Irish Music band and repairs musical instruments.

Simon Grenville is a former management trainee with the Orbit Housing Association concerned with rehousing the homeless in Milton Keynes and Central London. He is one the founding members of the Islington Community Housing Co-operative, North London, the East-West Theatre Company (Geoffrey Ost Memorial Award, University of Sheffield 1980) and the Alexandra Kollantai Film Corporation (2017). Currently trending on the Really TV Channel as Detective Inspector Paul Jones in Nurses Who Kill, Episode 1, Director Chris Jury. Training: Rose Bruford College.

Kate A.Harris and her three siblings lived on their farm near Market Harborough. She left home at 16 to pursue her career with children. After training in the Morley Manor, Dr. Barnardo's Home, in Derbyshire from 1966 to 1968, she qualified as a Nursery Nurse. Kate met and married her Royal Naval husband in Southsea when working in a children's home. As a naval wife, she was in Malta for two years with her two sons when they were shutting the naval base. They have two sons and two grandchildren. She worked on the local newspaper and discovered a love of writing at 50! Now she is writing her story mainly featuring Barnardo's. It's a major challenge with intense and fascinating research. She's had an incredible response from diverse and fascinating resources. Kate is interested in hearing from people who worked in Barnardo's, mainly in the 1960s.

Jim Hicks was born and raised in Rugby. After leaving school, he studied computing at Imperial College, London and the University of Cambridge. He worked in the Computing Services department of the University of Warwick for nearly twenty-six years before being made redundant in 2011.
His mother is a little surprised that he joined a writers' group. He thought someone might want some help with the technical side of using a computer to prepare documents, and has remained ever since.

Geoff Hill is a Zimbabwean writer and journalist living in Johannesburg. He is chief Africa Correspondent for The Washington Times (DC) and maintains a second home in Rugby. In 2000, Geoff became the first non-American to receive a John Steinbeck award for his writing. He has authored two books on Zimbabwe and writes for The Spectator.

John Howes was born and raised in Rugby. He was a journalist on local newspapers for 25 years before retraining as a teacher. He has self-published two books – We Believe, a collection of his writings on spirituality, and a guide on how to teach poetry. He plays the piano and writes music for schools and choirs. John is working on a memoir and dabbles in poetry. He runs a book group and is a member of St Andrew's Community Choir. He presents a Youtube Channel on the music of Elton John.

Ruth Hughes was born in Sutton Coldfield but has lived in Rugby for 50 years. She says, "I think I have a book in me but so far I just enjoy writing poems and recollections of my life." Ruth belongs to Murder 57, which enacts murder mysteries around the country, and to Rugby Operatic Society.

Sylvia Mandeville knew from a very young age that she wanted to be a poet, but Life and All That rather got in the way. It was not until much later, when living in Wales the land of bards, that she began to write poetry. Hopefully, a move to friendly and fascinating Rugby will continue to inspire!!!

Keith Marshall was educated at Cambridge and the Polytechnic of Central London. He worked in production management and human resources in the chemical industry before becoming a consultant management trainer in computers, working in Europe and Africa. He worked in race relations before setting up his own redundancy counselling business, finally specialising in secondary and higher education. As a volunteer, he has been an assessor of hospital care and has facilitated a mental health support group. Within a limited budget, he is a collector of porcelain and watercolours.

Madalyn Morgan was brought up in a pub in Lutterworth, where she has returned after living in

London for thirty-six years. She had a hairdressing salon in Rugby before going to Drama College. Madalyn was an actress for thirty years, performing on television, in the West End and in Repertory Theatre. She has been a radio journalist and is now presenting classic rock on radio. She has written articles for music magazines, women's magazines and newspapers. She now writes poems, short stories and novels. She has written ten novels – a wartime saga and a post war series. She is currently writing her memoir and a novel for Christmas 2023.

Steve Redshaw was born and raised in Sussex. Over the past forty years he has taught young children in the South of England and East Anglia. He has now retired and is living aboard his narrowboat, Miss Amelia, on the Oxford Canal near Rugby. His passion is music, singing and playing guitar, and various other plucked instruments, in pubs, folk clubs and sessions around the area. He also is a dance caller for Barn Dances and Ceilidhs. His creative output is perhaps best described as emergent and sporadic, but when time allows, he enjoys composing songs and writing short stories.

Chris Rowe. Just before covid, Chris tried to write poetry: lockdown gave the time to attempt different poetic forms - even a sonnet. Some of the poems here reflect past interests, in more agile days, of fell-walking and cross-country skiing, and Chris is currently a hard-put-upon housekeeper to a rescue cat. From childhood Chris has been interested in reading prose: such as Richmal Crompton (Just William), Alison Utley (Sam Pig), Henry Fielding, Mark Twain, Jane Austen, and Terry Pratchett.

Shakespeare has always been a favourite and long ago the ambition was achieved of seeing a performance of every play: Antony and Cleopatra being the hardest to track down (all those scene changes deter production.). Favourite performers of the Bard are Oddsocks.

Linda Slate has lived in Rugby for 11 years. She has 4 children, 15 grandchildren and 3 great-grandchildren. She has worked as a teacher and a police officer, both jobs have given her inspiration for her writing. Along with swimming, writing has been a lifelong passion. She has not yet had a novel published, but hopes to have one ready to submit by the end of 2023.

Sophie Walters is a member of Rugby Cafe Writers.

Lindsay Woodward has had a lifelong passion for writing, starting off as a child when she used to write stories about the Fraggles of Fraggle Rock. Knowing there was nothing else she'd rather study, she did her degree in writing and has now turned her favourite hobby into a career. She writes from her home in Rugby, where she lives with her husband and cat. When she's not writing, Lindsay runs a Marketing Agency, where she spends most of her time copywriting, so words really are her life. Her debut novel, Bird, was published in April 2016, and Lindsay's 9th novel is due to be released in 2023.

Chris Wright says the following:
My earliest memory is of my mother using flashcards to teach me to read while still in my playpen
we lived in a flat at West Heath,